Ketchup

Ketchup

Shazia Azhar MBE

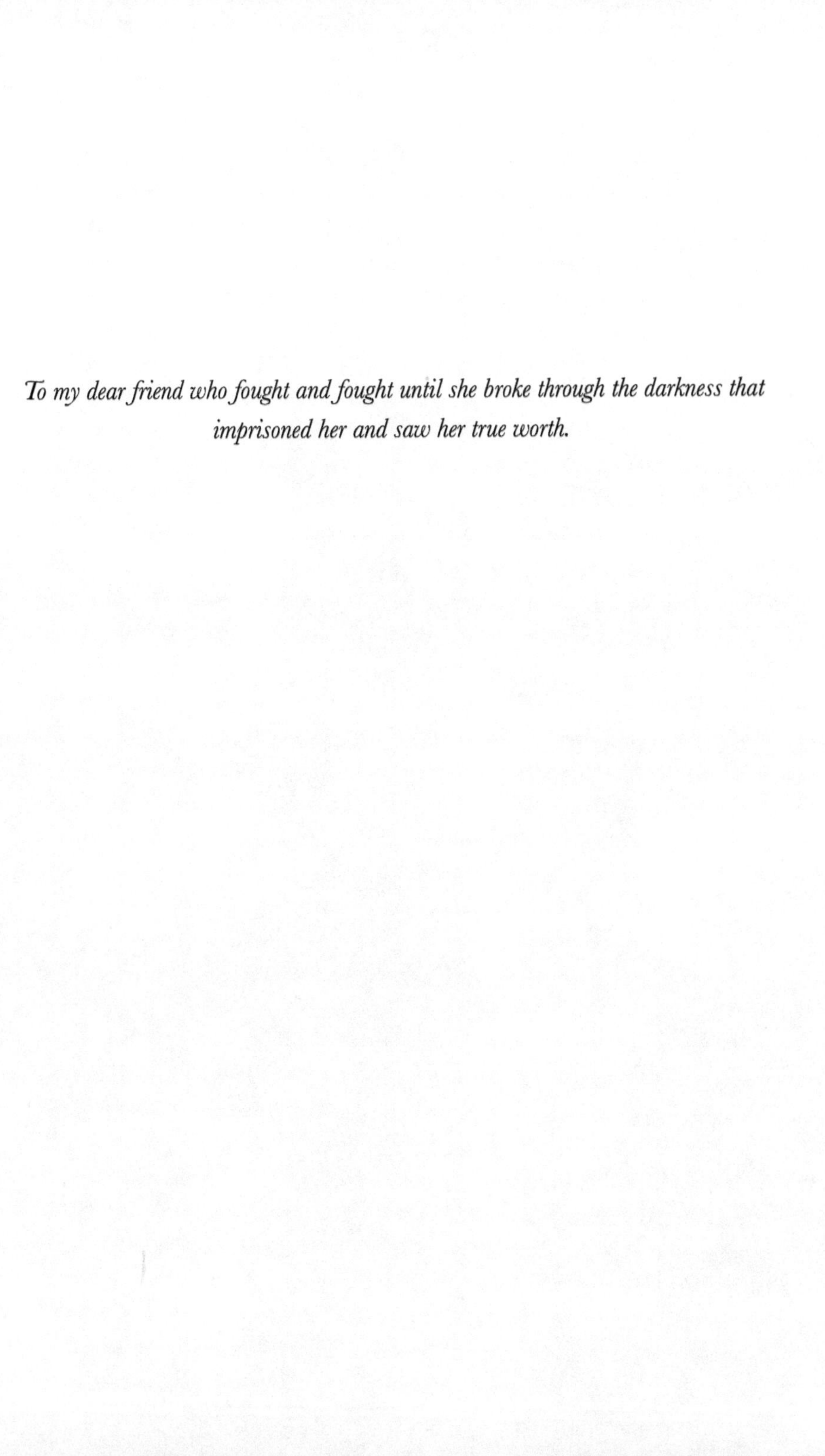

To my dear friend who fought and fought until she broke through the darkness that imprisoned her and saw her true worth.

I was the boss, a consummate professional. I noticed talent, productivity and output. So focused that I ignored the 'between the lines' information that wasn't business-related and sidestepped the gossip until, one day, I was in the eye of the storm.

"I need a day or two off; I'm sorry but it's for a court case and I'm a witness," she said as her eyes told a different story. She was worried that I would ask why or maybe she wanted me to. In any case, I didn't.

"That's fine. I understand you have to go. I've done jury service, too. It's a good experience," I said. I'm embarrassed now – I read it totally wrong and had no idea of what was to come.

I didn't hear anything more and I didn't even ask her how her time in court had gone. That was our only extended contact until she came into work two months later with a bruise on the right side of her face, along the jawline. The others fussed around her and came to me, "She's been attacked, Boss; she didn't want to say anything but she's in a state. Thought you should know." That's where it began.

"Come into my office," I smiled. She appeared nervous despite attempting to show some of her usual bravado – just a barrier, a front, I would soon learn. She told me that a man stalking her had attacked her. She said he was the reason for the court case.

She was intense, looking straight back at me as if she was looking for a reaction – but I didn't react – I listened. She told me that a man she knew had hit her, that her jaw had a fine fracture but that it would heal by itself over time. That she was fine and that the police were dealing with it. She asked me to circulate a photo of him just in case he turned up at the office. I agreed.

That day I held a team meeting. I passed a piece of paper around to the staff – it had a small photograph on it, not amazing quality, printed from the web. I remember vividly how she pulled back sharply, eyes widened and face filled with fear as the piece of paper passed her – she didn't touch it, her terror clear. The pressures of the job meant that we couldn't talk for long so I told her I was there if she needed anything and left it at that, but those words were new to her. She needed someone to listen and I did. We were always short of time so we would meet when possible, but when we couldn't meet at all or only for a short time we would continue via texts, thousands of texts.

We called the first exchange: **Day One**.
Zuby: https://www.victimsupport.org.uk/help-and-support/get-help/supportline. Have you seen this 👉 ?

Reena: I have now, thank you.

Zuby: Use it, pls.

Reena: I shall, promise.

Zuby: You were terrified when that photo passed you. Never seen you like that.

Reena: Sorry.

Zuby: No, no, I'm just concerned, that's all. Take care; see you tomorrow.

Day Two

It was the weekend and that Sunday morning we walked together for the first time. A walk that ended up being unexpectedly short in distance because we had to stop several times so that she could compose herself. She began to tell me about a monster. We didn't know each other well enough to share deeply, so as the days passed, texts made it easier, made us feel safe to talk.

> Reena: Thank you for caring, but please don't worry – I am tired and I am looking over my shoulder but I'm OK. Without sounding daft, I guess I'm used to dealing with rubbish situations and on my own x

Zuby: We'll talk tomorrow. I know you're strong but for your own long-term health, you need to allow someone who is an expert to help you – hence the numbers.

> Reena: I am going to use them, I promise x

Day Three

A friend and I had arranged to meet up with Reena for a Sunday afternoon cup of tea and perhaps even a slice of cake. The time approached.

> Reena: I'm really sorry, is there any chance of rescheduling today or you two going without me? I've spoken to Victim Support and the fear and stress is making me feel physically poorly – I just can't face the coffee shop x I do really want to see you both but I think I'll feel better another day. Sorry xx

Zuby: Reena, come to my house? I'll come and pick you up if it helps.

> Reena: That sounds more manageable if you
> honestly don't mind? I'll be OK to drive xx

Our friend couldn't make it now that the time had changed so for the first time I met Reena in my house. It was a little formal but she began to open up a little, so it seemed. I listened and told her it wasn't her fault and that he had no right. She said he had pushed her so hard she had a damaged rotator cuff, that her jaw hurt and that she couldn't eat the biscuits I had offered her. For the first time she told me that he called her names but she couldn't tell me what; the words wouldn't flow.

We seemed to save the difficult words for texts. I got it though, and I thought I could help a person running away from a man who made her feel as if she was worthless.

Day Four

> Reena: Drs didn't go great and conversation with
> Mum ended in WWIII again. Ah well, I tried x

Zuby: I'm sorry. You've got to focus on what you can
control and not worry about the things you can't. So
leave your mum for now, at least she knows.

Zuby: What's the dr saying? Are you booked in yet?

> Reena: I got in to the drs, given me an X-ray form
> to have jaw X-rayed again x I spoke through the
> situation and said I feel constantly on edge, it's
> brought up emotions and memories from the past.
> She said she doesn't want to give me anything
> chemical based at my age and the support I have

sounds sufficient – if I feel the same in a few weeks then go back and will see x

Zuby: It is a positive from the doctor. Shows she (with all her expertise) feels you have what you need in place. And like I said, we all have things in our lives we can't control. BTW, did I mention, writing down your feelings is another support mechanism, so might be worth a try?

Reena: The caseworker mentioned that x Thank you.

Zuby: I'm busy tomorrow but I'll be around Friday pm if you need to talk at all.

Reena: ☺

Day Five

Zuby: So, how are you doing today? Have you been for your X-ray?

Reena: OK today, thank you x Yes, said that it has moved – what was a hairline crack is now a break – have to go back in a week for another X-ray. It will heal naturally; if they're not happy then will look at surgery or wiring x Very soft/liquid diet for a week x

Zuby: Yuk, sounds sore. Stick to the liquid diet – get your blender out!

Reena: Time to get creative with soups x😋

Zuby: Reena, you need to acknowledge how you feel, accept that it is normal and then you can begin to learn to deal with it.

> Reena: It is nice to know that it's normal and I'm not overreacting x

Zuby: Exactly. It is good to distract yourself at times but ultimately you have to acknowledge how you feel. You are normal. Be kind to yourself.

That was the first time I had used that phrase: 'Be kind to yourself'. Subsequently, I used it countless times because she found that part so difficult.

Day Six

> Reena: Please can I work from home to go for my appointment tomorrow morning? Should be in by 10?

Zuby: Yes, looked pretty sore today.

> Reena: It's not great but will hopefully improve soon. Coughing didn't help it 😵. A few people saw it today :/ I said I fell in the bathroom 😖

Zuby: You know, you might consider telling people. They're a good bunch and would most likely look out for you.

> Reena: Hmm, they are a lovely bunch but I'm not sure I could hack all the sympathy.

Zuby: I can understand that. See how you feel in time.

Later…

Zuby: Right, be practical: write down what your worries/anxieties are, then write down how likely those are to materialise; finally, write down ways of dealing with those worries should they happen. Just talk to the support worker when you're anxious or not feeling yourself. Remember the short-term stresses must be addressed to make sure you're well in the long term.

Reena: Thank you.

Zuby: No need. Just speak to someone. I don't think you're in a position to make judgements about yourself. Let others help and make suggestions, then obviously you decide to take it or leave it.

Reena: I'm aiming to touch base with her once a week, no matter what, and then any more if I need and she's happy with that.

Day Seven

Zuby: How are you doing today?

Reena: On somewhat of a downward spiral today unfortunately, but thank you for asking x Have a lovely family gathering :)

Reena: I came home to a 3-page letter about how everything is my fault, I deserve everything I get, and will get, and I deserve everything that's coming.

Zuby: And you gave it to the police?

No answer…

Zuby: Do you want to talk about it?

Reena: No, nothing in particular. I think 'it' is frustration of having to deal with something again.

Zuby: You need to spend time with your thoughts when they occur and you need strategies to get through the negative feelings. First you have to accept them. Did you call the support people?

Reena: Yes, I spoke to someone – my usual person wasn't there – but the one I spoke to was nice; she did lots of listening and validating. Not a great evening 😠

Zuby: …and without justice first time round?

Reena: I think so, yes.

Zuby: *justice/closure/acknowledgement of wrongdoing.

Reena: Yes. I think it's different from anger, similar, but anger isn't right. I think it's frustration and what you said.

Zuby: Anger is linked to a feeling of loss of control.
The upset and tears = frustration at never having
him say sorry to you (I think).

Reena: I'm not sure it's so much of an apology I
feel is missing, more just completely got away with,
I think.

Zuby: Why don't you start by writing down what
you have felt over the last few days, and your related
reactions?

Reena: Will try.

Zuby: But this time – listen to your subconscious.
Chaos is tiring. I hope you can begin to make sense
of it now.

Reena: Dad is out a bit this weekend so I'll definitely
have some time to sit down with it: have e-mailed
Safeline, Carefirst? Will find somewhere/someone
soon.

Day Eight

Reena: Leeds tonight. Focus on you and your loved
ones, Zuby xx

Zuby: Glad you're out and about. Right, will leave
you alone.

Reena: With Dad at the hospital.

Zuby: Sorry, hope he's OK.

Reena: Focus is on Dad at the mo, but I did ring the number you gave me.

Zuby: All you need to know is that when there are highs and lows, and we know there are more of both to come, we are here; I am here. Please, please keep talking and be the person you want to be.

Reena: Thank you, you've been amazing!

Reena: I'm sat in Leeds waiting for Dad to wake up at the min x

Zuby: How's he doing?

Reena: Sleeping! Lazy so-and-so! Today's procedure went well, just keeping an eye now.

Zuby: That's good. Let the man rest. He'll be pleased you're there when he wakes.

Later…

Zuby: You looked drained today. Your dad needs you to be well so you can look after him.

Reena: I thought I looked better today! Ha ha. Just been kicked out of the hospital 😳. Txt when I get home.

On an evening Reena would write down her thoughts and any new learning on a large sheet of paper. She would send me the images of her writing for us to discuss.

Zuby: I'm worried about you. I don't think you've even contacted the counsellors?

> Reena: Yes, I did; the number you gave me wasn't for them but I got through in the end and spoke to someone. They don't do f2f though – just a free 30min and then a contracted 6hrs. She doesn't think they're suitable for me though :/

Zuby: I'm worried that if you don't access these services now you will find it difficult to deal with whatever the future brings. Does that make sense?

> Reena: Complete sense.

Zuby: Good, then do the A3 sheet when you are in the right frame of mind.

> Reena: That's the messy corner – emotions/ reactions that I've yet to file somewhere. Copy/ send/tell and I'll resign.

Zuby: I do not tell others what I have discussed with you or anyone else unless I have permission first. Integrity.

> Reena: Telling someone how you're feeling when you: A) don't fully know, and B) have hidden it so long is scary. I am trying – you've got more out of

me than anyone ever has. I wholly appreciate your support, I cannot explain how much.

Day Nine

Zuby: You didn't say, what happened at the police station?

Reena: He's going for an 'unfit to plead' 😖 Getting particularly tired and fed up.

Zuby: Here's the plan: 1) deal with the historic issues. Accept that they happened and, importantly, understand that they can never happen to you again.

Zuby: Why did you refer to him as an ex before? Not so if he groomed you??

Reena: When I mentioned the historical stuff on the phone she asked me if I had reported it and what had happened. Habit, I guess; was 18 before I escaped – I won't again.

Zuby: Excellent. Then do you think you can let the injustice and emotions around that go?

Reena: Yes. The emotions and anything to do with injustice, yes. It's the ashamed that's harder.

Zuby: Why? You were a child.

Reena: I'll deal with that. What's part 2?

Zuby: P2) you take control of the current situation with him.

Reena: By..?

Zuby: You are clear in your head that he cannot harm you physically or otherwise. You will take your self-defence classes and if he comes near you, you know he'll regret it. You hope the court case happens quickly and he goes to jail but you do not plan your life waiting for that to happen. If it doesn't, it doesn't.

Reena: In black and white that sounds great. However... he can physically harm me if he gets hold of me again. This isn't up to me☹.

Zuby: Part 3) focus on the parts that are.

Reena: I can't talk at the minute, I'm in the middle of screaming and shouting and balling but I really, really don't want to take it out on you. I'm trying, I'm really, really trying, but I can't and won't get it all right first time round, but I am listening and I am trying.

Zuby: Finally, you admit it. That's fine. Accept it's OK not to get everything right first time and admit it to yourself instead of trying to put up a false abrasive front.

Reena: I don't know of any other front and right now I need a front.

Zuby: No, you don't need that defensive, negative, false front because I can see right through it. All I'm saying is focus on those things and that will help you to deal with but not eliminate the other things. Be in control. Focus on the positives this week. It's the way to get through this – you're a survivor, not a victim.

Reena: I think it's because it's been a tough week emotionally and being here without Dad brings it home. I usually try and do something (read, plan, sort) to switch my focus but I couldn't successfully do any.

Zuby: OK, try and do something for yourself. If you need to talk, walk or anything else, I'm here.

Day Ten

Reena: Will go to the hospital soon.

Zuby: I know I make it all sound so easy as I know it's very difficult in your shoes, but give yourself time to try these strategies as I know you will be where you want to be in those next 5 years we spoke about.

Reena: What you say does make sense and I do do it; I will focus on keeping them up. Thank you for your time.

Zuby: One other question remains – that's the blame question, which is clearly a major drain on you. All I can say here is that a perpetrator of violence and grooming – an adult – is the ONLY one who is to blame.

Reena: Hopefully the f2f will help with that. I say it until I'm blue in the face but I don't necessarily believe it. But I can park it while I deal with what and who's important.

Zuby: I'm going to make it my mission to make sure you get there.

Reena: I will.

Day Eleven

Zuby: 'Instead of seeing ourselves as a problem to be fixed... SELF-kindness/compassion allows us to see ourselves as valuable human beings who are worthy of care.'[1] You need to judge yourself in the same way you would a child going through the same sort of trauma.

Reena: What book is that from? I wondered if you'd suggest it that way.

Zuby: Is that a helpful way to suggest it? Not from a book. You've achieved a lot of this but you clearly haven't forgiven yourself yet. Please do.

Reena: I am trying and I am willing to keep trying until I genuinely get there. This is the closest I've ever been – honestly, Zuby – and it is down to you and your time you've dedicated.

Zuby: I know you are. I don't mean for you to do it all now. Give yourself a break.

Reena: We were close today and I was ready to say stop but then it calmed down.

Zuby: OK, just remember I'm not trained; I'm sort of guessing (educated guesses).

Reena: I know, very brave of you to do so, and I do hugely appreciate all of your time and effort.

Zuby: Any news on your X-ray?

Reena: To have a plate put in, it's healing wrong. They will ring me with an appointment. I can't help being miffed about it but I'm trying to be outwardly positive.

Zuby: Anyone would be.

Reena: I'm definitely apprehensive and it's more the counselling tomorrow. I don't know where it's going to go and there are some places I purposely haven't been to in a long time. Hoping tomorrow is a fairly 'easy' first appointment.

Zuby: Don't tell me there's more?!

Reena: Gosh, no! There's no more. I'm sure tomorrow will be OK anyway.

Zuby: They won't be judging, so be honest with yourself and the counsellor. Good luck.

Day Twelve

> Reena: Feel very sick :(

Zuby: This is an opportunity. Be positive.

We met briefly after the appointment to talk about the format of the session and to reassure each other.

> Reena: EMDR sounds awful, effective but I'm steamrollered ☺

Zuby: You should be proud of what you achieved today.

> Reena: I will be. I've gone funny now I'm home; just can't put my finger on what but I'll be fine.

Zuby: BTW it's at least 5 positives to cancel out every 1 negative.

> Reena: Not as hard as you first made it sound then ☺

Zuby: Positive comments and conversations produce a chemical reaction, too. They stir the production of oxytocin impacting our prefrontal cortex.

> Reena: You sound like the woman this morning.

Zuby: Promise me one thing: you have to tell me when I'm pushing too hard.

> Reena: I did get close to saying stop today but then didn't need to, honest.

> Reena: And today began with being tough because we went right back, and that's not pleasant, but we didn't stay there long so it was manageable.

> Reena: This is my next read according to the counsellor.

The book that had been recommended was about men that abuse and their reasons for doing so.

Zuby: You need to understand yourself first, not him!

> Reena: She said a lot; I can't remember all of it as I was still trying to process and listen at the same time.

Zuby: She's there to help you. Nothing wrong with taking notes.

> Reena: I'll go with notebook in hand next time.

Zuby: Yes, and stop her to ask questions, if you need to. Ah, I think I know why. Stats show that people in violent/abusive relationships may be susceptible to future similar relationships – unless they recognise the signs.

Day Thirteen

I asked Reena to carry out a task in a different way to improve performance at work but she didn't react well and had defended her actions in a verbally aggressive manner. I responded by clearly stating what I had requested and then left the room. As ever, discussions couldn't happen then and there due to the need to continue with the business of the day. We texted late into the evening.

> Reena: I'm sorry about my outburst.

Zuby: Now you mention it, I did have to defend
myself quite rigorously on a Friday afternoon in
front of lots of people, and that's why you should
keep trying to make sure it doesn't happen again.

> Reena: I think I was bang out of order and I didn't
> like it, I deserved a serious dressing-down. Wish it
> hadn't come to that but it has given me a shock and
> was a realisation of how I need to really deal with
> things because they manifest in other potentially
> damaging ways.

Zuby: We can walk on Sunday and maybe talk it
through. My concern is that you go a little too far in
front of others – I would need to address it because
otherwise it would undermine me.

> Reena: I know. I am consciously working on it.

Zuby: Glad you realise that but you need to do that
before it happens. Not so helpful a couple of hours
later. You still behave like a teenager sometimes.

> Reena: 😳 Sorry x

Zuby: Focus on the learning path – from disappointment through to how you feel in that moment – to how you will react in a proportionate way.

> Reena: I shall, I shall. I'm really disgusted at myself and it was a shock I (shouldn't have) needed.

Zuby: This is where you have to forgive yourself instead of being so harsh. It's OK, no big deal. I'm going to send that YouTube video I've been talking about. It's tough in places so note the following BEFORE you watch it: 1) you are not to blame; 2) neurological changes have taken place in your brain and that is why there is no quick fix (I get that now); 3) if you do not deal with this now, it will impact on your future; 4) you can resolve this so that your future is not dictated by your past, and 5) you are not alone. (https://www.ted.com/talks/nadine_burke_harris_how_childhood_trauma_affects_health_across_a_lifetime)

> Reena: Right then. In a nutshell, scuppered.

Zuby: No, not at all.

Zuby: So, you can stop blaming yourself. It's official; it's science.

> Reena: Remember when I was really suffering with my headaches and had all the scans, etc? It was my pituitary gland then, weird.

Zuby: Yes, I thought the same. Makes sense, doesn't it?

Reena: Definitely interesting.

Zuby: Remember the key messages: there's hope; there are solutions.

Reena: It would be nice to be normal without having to work so chuffing hard at it ☹

Zuby: I was hoping you might be more positive about its message.

Reena: Sorry, I like the facts and the figures and the physiological impact that happens as a result of the events and not the individual – it's good validation that things are as a result of that and not of me.

Zuby: You are where you are. What had happened to you shouldn't have but no one can change that. By taking back control, you can stop the long-term impact. She sees it as a treatable condition. She acknowledges that childhood trauma runs into adulthood. Explains your behaviour totally.

Reena: I will see this through; without intending to sound pathetic – working to stop the long term impact is a 24/7 job, trying to make sure a decision is by me, for me, and for the right reasons, working at always moving forwards and being conscious of how I am whilst trying to cover it so I seem normal – is exhausting. I'll deal with it and process it and move on from it – I will, but it ain't gonna be done overnight.

Zuby: It is exhausting because you are essentially trying to reprogramme your brain. You don't sound pathetic, just like someone in pain, someone who is struggling but determined. I get that.

Reena: That's why I withdraw when I do because, sometimes, the covering up is just one step too far.

Zuby: I understand. It's about the future, your 5-year plan. Now, did you notice the part about future relationships?

Reena: Yes...

Zuby: About behaviours being repeated?

Reena: I'm aware. And that's why counselling is one of the steps towards that.

Zuby: You repeatedly apologise for things that aren't your fault and over-apologise when they are. I think, if someone wanted to, they could take advantage of that obvious low self-esteem and vulnerability.

Reena: I hate hurting people. Ideally, in my future I'll have a family, but if that's not there I'd hoped a partner could be.

Zuby: There's no reason why you couldn't have a partner. I'm saying you must realise that because of

the behaviour I describe above, you are vulnerable
to manipulation. It's not just partners either, could
be anyone you interact with.

> Reena: I am aware that I am easy to manipulate
> and I know it's not a good thing. I guess the low
> self-esteem (don't like that either) is the reason
> I am more conscious of upsetting others than
> myself, although as I'm saying it, that could be a
> programmed safety response – safer for me to keep
> him happy than suffer the wrath.

> Reena: I'm known as the loud, confident, 'says what
> she thinks' one. But I hate myself when I'm how I
> was today.

Zuby: I told you, when you feel this way you have to
tell yourself repeatedly 'I will not be a victim.' No
one can help you until you help yourself.

> Reena: No one can; I will give as good as I can for
> as long as I can but there'll come a time when I'll
> crash and have no more to give – that's no one's
> fault and no one's responsibility to pick up the pieces
> from, it will just be.

Zuby: To reprogramme your brain, you need to see
your strategies and repeat them.

> Reena: Yes, the strategies are on my positive list. I'll
> be OK.

Zuby: Then, can you focus on just those positives?

> Reena: I'll try. It's really late and it's really not fair on you. Before you say it, you are helping, massively. I will be OK, just not all at once and not immediately.

Zuby: I'm giving you just one task today, if I may, then I'll get off your case for today. Will you pls note down every positive thing you achieve or do today? I would like a long list for tomorrow.

> Reena: Shall do: I can eat peaches 😃

Zuby: Be ready to walk and talk. Got a list of questions for you. I'm going to use the 80:20 rule for talk (you're the 80).

Zuby: Using positives is good for you, even when directed at others. As I said the other day, positive language releases certain chemicals in the brain.

Zuby: You are a good person who deserves good things and the future you wish for. You can change things to make that happen whilst ensuring you recognise and change the potential pitfalls.

> Reena: Thank you!

We walked that morning for a good couple of hours and Reena revealed some more detail about her childhood. She gave me enough detail for me to be able to research the feelings she was experiencing.

Day Fourteen

Zuby: Research done. Shows the following: talking therapies are extremely effective but only in certain situations. Here are the questions you need to answer to know if it will work for you: 1) Have you consigned the trauma to the past? (i.e. when you talk about it, you don't get the traumatic feelings anymore). If your answer is 'Yes' – no need to talk about it. If your answer is 'No' – talking will help. How? I hear you ask. When you talk about the event, you do it with someone guiding you through how to feel about it now. The science behind it: when we process events, our brain turns them into a narrative from the past by detaching the emotion from the event, so all the events are still there but you can talk about them without feeling afraid, etc. A trauma that isn't processed makes you feel all of the negative feelings you originally felt. It's like you are reliving it – not helpful at all. However, by talking it through and training the brain to process it, it becomes manageable.

> Reena: Hmm.

Zuby: Not clearly explained?

> Reena: Clearly explained. My situation is just so chuffing awkward that I can't work out which bits go where.

Zuby: Take your time and think about the above.
You'll know what you have to do next.

> Reena: It probably hasn't been processed. I had consigned it to the past and then the physical assault made me feel vulnerable again. I was a little angry on our walk when I mentioned feeling ashamed and pathetic for having to deal with it.

Zuby: Take a break. Go and do something nice for yourself. We don't need to have all the answers today. When you're ready, reply. Anytime is OK.

During the breaks from texting, I would read medical journals and research papers as well as the blogs of counsellors and survivors. Some aspects would click with the information Reena had shared with me so I would put them to her.

Zuby: Answer these questions to help you decide:
1) How do you feel on a typical day in school?
2) How do you feel on a typical day at home?
3) What is your self-talk on a typical day? (school/ home)
4) Stuck in childhood?
5) What next? Self-regulation, plan, monitor, evaluate and self-talk. You have to consciously go through this process, OK?
6) How will you guard against being manipulated?
7) What do you think you deserve?

Reena: 1) Confident, safe, purposeful, positive.
2) Afraid, alone, vulnerable.
3) Not sure what my self-talk is so I'm going to work on being more conscious of it.
4) Yes, physiological change. Work on stopping and thinking.
5) Future danger – health, relationships, children.
6) Be conscious of apologies – only when appropriate.
7) Family instead of being alone, career of own choice instead of job without prospects, safety instead of feeling at threat – nice things!

Zuby: Your mind remains in the traumatic time –
we have to help you to move on –reprogramming,
etc.

Zuby: When you talk about the event, you do it in
a calm manner with someone guiding you through
how you should feel now.

> Reena: I can speak about the events very matter-of-factly and detach emotions of fear and vulnerability from that time unless I'm being asked about recent events and the similarities/reminders that they bring.

> Reena: It's not a traumatic feeling when I'm talking about it. It's disgust and shame, yes, but not traumatic.

Zuby: But from this morning I know you don't truly
believe them. But it's progress.

Reena sent me a photo of her handwritten recollections. She described how he would use awful, derogatory terms towards her and how he would physically hurt her.

Zuby: I don't like what I'm reading. It's sad.

> Reena: 😔

Zuby: The situation at any given time may heighten
certain feelings from the past, but when your brain
has genuinely processed an event so that it becomes
no more than a narrative to acknowledge events

in your past, you will not feel the negative feelings anymore, just the sadness and the associated anger that it ever happened. The fact that you still vividly feel those things suggests to me that you do need to talk about the aspects that give you those particular feelings but not the rest.

> Reena: I'll see 🙁 Completely understand what you're saying.

The feelings of shame persisted and Reena brought it up many times during our walks, but I didn't understand. This was an area I knew very little about and, if I'm totally honest, I wanted Reena to tell me herself.

Zuby: Are you able to tell me? I don't understand this part. Especially as we've gone through so much of the other aspects including serious emotional aspects.

> Reena: You won't like it; you really won't like it. And as tough as you try to appear, you have really heartbreakingly sad eyes when something hits you.

Zuby: Then tell me via txt. I'm desperate to find an answer for you, for that part.

> Reena: You still won't like it. Spoken or written.

Zuby: I don't like anything I've heard, but I think we're past that. I feel like there is a missing piece of this jigsaw. I don't understand why you feel that way about yourself given everything you've said.

Reena: I guess when you've felt it for 12 years it's more of a habit? I'm referring to the blame.

Zuby: The research shows that people feel this way after the event but when it's been discussed with them, they learn that they were blameless. With you, you know you weren't to blame; you say you can talk the events through in a matter-of-fact way, suggesting your mind has processed it, but your sense of 'disgust' and 'shame' is still so strong.

Reena: I don't know what to say ☹

Zuby: Tell me why you use such strong adjectives to describe your feelings.

Reena: That is how I feel about it, Zuby. I hate that it happened.

Zuby: 'It' wasn't you.

Reena: The fact it happened is what makes me feel ashamed and as dirty as 'damaged goods' – you get the idea. I don't want sympathy and I'm not sure that bit can be fixed.

Zuby: Yes, it can, of that I'm certain and the research backs me. You were a child and you were afraid to say 'No'. I'm not giving you sympathy, I'm trying to help you ensure your future is what you deserve and not based on your past.

Reena: The learning not to blame myself bit is coming. I'm really. really working on it and regularly telling myself what the truth is.

Zuby: And what IS the truth?

Reena: That it wasn't my fault and I am not to blame.

Zuby: There is something/some reason you don't really believe that, though. What is it?

Reena: It is coming. I don't know what you want me to say ☹

Zuby: I want to know what happened that makes you think any of this is your fault.

Reena: Shame from sexual abuse can last far longer than any other damage. It seeps into your being. You fear what others might think if they knew. Even though, rationally, a now-adult victim realises that she was a trusting child, she's absorbed deep shame as if it were her fault.

Zuby: Forgive me. I'm sorry. I know it's none of my business but you've told me so much, I need to do something. I'm sorry if I've gone too far and upset you further.

Reena: You haven't x But once you know then you can't 'unknow' and you may wish that you could. There's 6 years of rubbish.

Zuby: My only aim is to try and find some answers.
There is nothing you could have done in your
childhood that would make me blame you. Same as
any other child's experiences I have ever dealt with,
in 25 years at work.

> Reena: I don't mean anything I did; there isn't
> anything else to add to my story.

That afternoon we met up at a local coffee shop. I looked at her
frail posture and shared my concerns. I told her that I really didn't
understand and wanted to so that I could help. She began to say
the words that would change everything for me and words that she
had never said to anyone else before. She looked at me intently for
a reaction and my shock must have been visible, but she had said
enough. She stopped as her eyes became teary and I reassured her.
We decided to stop there because we were both aware of the other
customers and what they might think.

Zuby: Tomorrow I will be able to look you in the eye
and respect you in the same way I always have done
as a good person. Nothing changes.

> Reena: ☺ I won't give up, I absolutely will not ever
> give up.

> Reena: I've written down the narrative – the parts I
> didn't say. If you want it I'll send it. You won't like it
> and I won't be offended if you stop reading part way
> through and delete it x

Zuby: I'm not as soft as you think.

Reena: When it started I was 13, looking after his son. He said it's what I wanted, that I'd been egging him on. The safeguarding warnings of new phones and flash gifts didn't happen, it was purely a mental load that I'd be the one in the wrong if anything came out.

At 15, people found out; I lost my friends at school, teachers shunned me and Mum kicked me out. Within a month I was living with him. He trained me in all the right things to say to which people. For the next few months I thought I was happy. Then the heavy drink started, the fierce control, the violence and accusations of ruining his life.

At 16, I was doing my GCSEs, following his rules, making sure I was home on time so he didn't kick off, having tea on the table for his son and helping him with his homework. I left school with 16 GCSEs.

When I left school I tried to get a job because he didn't like that I hadn't contributed to the running of the household (they don't pay child support to someone who isn't your carer, much to his dismay!) The first 2 jobs I started ended within a month due to violent accusations of relationships with the bosses. I eventually found a job I was allowed to have but obviously my money wasn't my own. I went to college, still making sure his son was being looked after and safe, and so I couldn't go to all the classes because he was my priority (the violence, accusations and alcohol addiction continued). I left college with 2 distinction level diplomas, 1 grade A A-level and an AS level.

University wasn't allowed at this point. His son went

to live with his own mum after I once stopped his dad attacking him. The violence, control and abuse got worse and I was regularly accused of seeing other people and therefore 'paying for it'. That's when I considered I'd be better off doing something silly.

At 18 (October), I escaped. I packed all I could into my car and ran. I came to Dad's. I briefly went back through fear and left for good in the December. The following 2 years I was stalked and harassed. I eventually pressed charges, took him to court and you know the rest. The February following the December I signed up to university.

Zuby: Thank you for telling me. This should never have happened to you. I know how I feel reading it. I hope you acknowledge how you feel and that your feelings are normal. You were never to blame.

Reena: Thank you.

Zuby: I don't have any words right now but I am here if you need me.

Reena: I'm sorry you don't have any words x I don't like it when you go quiet. It's OK, Zuby, I'm OK(ish) as it's not happening now and it's what I survived. And notice the theme throughout – what I achieved.

Zuby: I believe every word you've written. Your mum's a cow, though (sorry).

> Reena: Means a lot, thank you. Not arguing with you. I'm worried I've really upset you 🙁

Zuby: Please don't worry. Focus on you. I'm sorry I wasn't helpful today.

> Reena: You were helpful, you didn't judge! I'm sure you'll get me if and when you think of anything to say.

Day Fifteen

At work the next day, my silence continued. I didn't know what to say to be of any help and I really didn't want to say something ridiculous like 'It's all alright'. It was anything but, despite rehearsing the words for much of the day. Nothing seemed apt so I said nothing until later in the evening. Texts felt a little more manageable.

Zuby: I didn't want you to think I was avoiding you (which maybe I was). So what I have to say is this: society failed you – the school, your mum – those that should have looked after you turned away and failed you. They are the ones to blame – not you. The police, courts and any others who might have helped are to blame, not you. Most of all, HE is to blame. You are an amazing person to go against the statistics and achieve what you have done in so little time. You have nothing to be ashamed of because you are not the cause of any of what has happened to you. Hold your head up high and be proud of everything you have achieved and of the things you are going to achieve. I am so, so sorry you have had to endure all of this.

Reena: Aw Zuby, they are wonderful words, thank you x

Zuby: https://www.loveisrespect.org/wpcontent/uploads/2016/11/Power_And_Control.png. This is why it's his fault.

Reena: That's scary; was my life down to a tee.

Zuby: Going by our conversations, you have managed to rationalise everything that has happened to you, except the fault/self-blame aspect, so this is what we need to address. You can do it. I'm going to help you.

Reena: You have already helped so much more than you realise.

Zuby: I really hope so but to have impact on your future, we need to go further. You will not be that person that suffers in future because of their past. The focus has to be on 2 aspects now: 1) your dad; 2) rid yourself of the self-blame. The self-blame comes from wanting control. So by blaming yourself, you satisfy yourself (subconsciously), that you had control. To accept it wasn't your fault, you have to accept you're not always in control.

Reena: That does make sense because my line has always been that: 'I'm fine, it was my doing, I got myself into the situation', etc.

Zuby: So, do you think, despite being in control (except that you weren't), bad things happened so you must have deserved it, and that's where the low self-esteem comes from?

Reena: Deep down, yes, but I now know that it shouldn't be like that and I'm consciously working towards not blaming myself. Writing it down last night made me think – the instant reactions from friends, teachers and Mum were that it was my responsibility and I was in the wrong, was coupled with the years of blame I received from him.

Zuby: He was bound to blame you because he's a *@%**, friends blamed you because they were young and didn't understand what was happening.

Reena: Yes, I understand that. In their shoes it was easier to go their own ways than get caught up.

Zuby: I don't understand your mum's reaction, though. In any case, she shouldn't have abandoned you. She should have fought for you.

Reena: Apparently not all mums think like you.

Zuby: The school and the police were ignorant. They probably stereotyped. The courts were fooled. It happens all the time. That bit I know from personal experience.

Reena: That's such a simple thing and explains a lot.

Zuby: I hope now that you have some explanations
that make sense; you can note them on your piece
of paper.

Reena: Thank you. I'm a bit lost for words, not sure
what to say – it's quite a revelation. PS. I'm much
more at ease now you've found some words. You
threw me today.

Zuby: You should always be at ease. I can't help how
I react but I'm always on your side.

Reena: I didn't doubt that, just felt like I'd broken
you! I am sorry I brought this car crash to you.

Zuby: Keep talking, I'm still here when you need
me. You will not push me away, whatever.

Reena: You couldn't look at me. I'm not surprised;
it's fine. I've been living it for 12 years and it's still
c*** – you've known it for all of 2 days!

Zuby: I will tomorrow. I promise. I'm sorry I let you
down today. Won't happen again. The person who
listens to a survivor should not tell the survivor (or
show them) how they feel. This is because it will
add to feelings of fault and blame. So the last thing
I want is for you to worry about me. It is not your
fault. I will keep saying it.

Reena: In which case the survivor shouldn't speak
to a human being! Sitting back and thinking about
it, I think it's thrown me because no one has ever

reacted to me sympathetically, everyone reacted in the opposite way.

Zuby: When I feel upset it is not because I am judging you or blaming you at all. You see that, don't you?

Reena: I do, it's just not easy seeing someone upset about your circumstances (you wouldn't be upset if you didn't know). And this next bit is going to sound selfish and stupid but I'm going to say it anyway... there's a part of me that thinks, 'Why couldn't someone have responded that way all those years ago?'

Zuby: I don't know how to respond except that I'm not supposed to be upset in front of you because you might think I'm blaming you. I failed that one but I honestly don't blame you.

Day Sixteen

We both had a productive day at work, focused on the job with the odd innocuous interaction. After hours, I looked at Reena's latest set of notes and began texting.

Zuby: Managed to look you in the eye today.

Reena: You did, you are helping a lot, I promise.

Zuby: Now, the reprogramming. What was actually happening? Who was to blame? It makes me feel physically sick, reading this. It's clear who's to

blame, who is guilty and who should be ashamed.
It's NOT you.

> Reena: I'm not sure I'll be able to do any processing
> or dealing with tonight. I'm very much in fight-or-
> flight mode.

Zuby: That's fine but come out of that fight-or-flight
mode. You know you're safe so you can take control
of how you deal with the evening ahead. You wrote
'food' on your sheet. Is it still an issue?

> Reena: No, can cross off; I'm getting better and
> making a conscious effort to eat.

Zuby: You seem to have lost weight to me. You need
to keep a check.

> Reena: I have lost weight ☹ but I'm working on it.

Zuby: Thought so. You look gaunt, too. Physically,
you need to look after yourself. Remember, you can't
let the bastards win. You have to do everything in
your power to take control where you can.

> Reena: Lost weight, gaunt – anything else? I am
> trying; I am eating. Soups aren't the most fattening
> of meals!

Zuby: I want to go through the parts you circled and
reassert how to address those areas. Not sure it'll
work via txt but can try. Now that I can look at you

again, it's helpful to read your expression. Txts don't
tell the whole truth.

> Reena: I try; sometimes it'll take a while for me to think of the right words.

Zuby: You circled: 'anger/ashamed – loss of control'.
Deal with the ashamed part. Repeat why this isn't the
case.

> Reena: I can't. Concern about Dad – home alone a lot so fearful, coming to terms with not having control – could really do with having a mum or older sister figure right now when I can't burden Dad and they're sodding sh*te.

Zuby: But you have others now.

> Reena: I know, I know, but it's not chuffing fair on every poor soul that I'm burdening with this cr*p, people have normal lives. Then when those people look at me they see the broken bits and not what they did before. So much of me wishes that I'd kept it from school and then people wouldn't know any different.

Zuby: That was your choice and theirs. No one has to
engage if they don't want to.

> Reena: Sorry, I think I'm more irate than usual this evening – fear from the attack coupled with genuine realisation that there were people back down the line who should have done more when they could have been able to impact the situation.

Zuby: The realisation is good. Will help you understand it wasn't ever your fault.

> Reena: It doesn't have good effects immediately; I'm just livid and hurt at the min.

Zuby: Deal with the ashamed part. Repeat why that should not be the case. Use any vocab you need to.

> Reena: I wasn't in control; I was picked out and manipulated. I was young and impressionable. I was coerced and groomed and when I was where he wanted me he didn't need the nice persona. The people who could have helped chose not to; they stereotyped and rinsed their hands as quickly as they could.

Zuby: Correct, and do you believe this? ☝

> Reena: Yes… and then I think I was f***ing stupid for not seeing through it earlier 😖 I am trying so hard to genuinely and wholly believe it, I really am.

Zuby: You were not stupid. How could you have seen through such manipulation when you were a child, expecting those around you to be trustworthy? You must believe it.

> Reena: I'm being honest with you. I could easily say I believe it and not mean it but that's not what you've asked for.

Zuby: I don't want you to pretend. To do you any good, you truly have to believe it. I'm trying to help you to rewire. I know it will take time. I'm hoping we're making progress.

> Reena: We are.

Zuby: I'll keep repeating it till I feel silly, but I'm not giving up. And neither are you. You must stop using derogatory terms about yourself (stupid, apologetic, etc).

> Reena: Noted. I'll try.

Zuby: You underlined 'physical' – tell me about that.

> Reena: My face bloody hurts. In a nutshell. PS. I'm ringing up tomorrow morning about op.

Zuby: I know, but you had countered it to say it was fixable. This was one area you appeared to deal with well.

> Reena: I circled bits that were still affecting me; it's still affecting me in that it hurts. It is fixable (without counselling) and will be fixed properly soon.

Zuby: It's OK to be cross, it's a normal reaction to the 💩 you've been through. But If you can be calm in the moment (after your initial reaction, you will reduce the release of harmful chemicals into your body. I've had a knot in my chest for a few days; it's quite tiring. I expect you have that all the time.

Reena: 😞 I didn't plan to give you a taste of my life, but yes. I will find some appropriate relaxation exercises for you. OK, here goes: 'Ashamed' – you underlined that a second time elsewhere on the sheet. Tell me why you don't need to again.

Reena: I wasn't in control; I was picked out and manipulated. I was young and impressionable. I was coerced and groomed and when I was where he wanted me he didn't need the nice persona. The people who could have helped chose not to; they stereotyped and rinsed their hands as quick as they could.

Zuby: Process the thought and then write it – 'reprogramming'.

Reena: I wasn't to blame. I was groomed and controlled. I was let down by those who could have helped. But in trying to deal with the past a lot of that has come to the forefront, coupled with the git who thinks he's above the law. When this bit is over I am hoping some of the historic parts can be put to bed.

Zuby: Another job for tomorrow – ring the police and ask if you can have an alarm at home. You're safe with Scott there. Try and rest. If you do, it will set you up for a good day tomorrow. One day at a time.

Reena: Dad has some sleeping tabs in the cupboard, considering those and Horlicks.

Zuby: Try and sleep. I'll leave you alone but I'm awake if you do want to talk.

> Reena: Thank you, Zuby.

Day Seventeen

> Reena: Got a pre-op appointment.

Zuby: When is it likely to be?

> Reena: Police said that the alarm isn't something they do directly; it's through Victim Support.

Zuby: OK, and talking of Victim Support – have you contacted them?

> Reena: That's tomorrow's job.

Zuby: They're open till 8. Do it now.

She said she would and I believed her. Her texts suggested she really had.

> Reena: They laughed at me 😠 I'll speak to Rachel about exactly what it's called tomorrow. Actually, I'll e-mail her now.

Zuby: Laughed at you? Why?

> Reena: Because the attacker hasn't been in the house or attacked the house and 'it doesn't work like American films'.

Zuby: OMG, what is wrong with these people?

Reena: It's not my fault, it's not my fault, it's not my fault, it's not my fault.

Zuby: It is not, Reena. Are you alright? Don't get dragged down by this. You're still at the hospital so you're safe right now. Try and think about what we said this morning. Take any moments of peace.

Reena: Yes, going for Matt now.

Zuby: Basically, neuroplasticity can be applied to help you manage, treat and perhaps even 'cure' anxiety, but it takes some time and effort! These more permanent brain changes can be achieved through adapting and changing thought patterns through recall, breathing exercises, increasing body awareness and targeting sensory perception. Neuroplasticity = rewiring your brain.

Reena: Thank you. Did that account for years of being f***ed up?

Zuby: You have to use positive self-talk repeatedly. Not language like the above, which is negative.

Reena: Old habits die hard 😳

Zuby: Seriously though, you can change your future.

Reena: I will.

Zuby: So spend some time every day seizing the moments that are positive. It's in your control.

Reena: Thank you :)

Zuby: Remember to write down all of the positives for today and go through the self-talk.

Day Eighteen

In line with our new morning routine (weather permitting), we would go for a long walk and talk about the situation. We would reflect and absorb what had happened and then text each other.

Zuby: Research proves that it takes 10–20 seconds for a positive feeling to be absorbed by the brain, to record it into a deeper neural structure. In recovery you want as many of those experiences as possible as you retrain and rewire the brain to release fear and hypervigilance, embracing safety, calmness and control. Healing is hard and messy and often feels really, really crappy. You may get worse for a while instead of better. You may feel better, have a triggering episode and think you've lost ground. You may experience all of these things and then decide it's not worth the fight. Still, it wouldn't be because your brain wasn't willing. It would be because you weren't. Summary of this morning:
* It's exhausting to consciously implement all of the strategies discussed so we need to recoup energy in some way (every good moment is recognised and used to remove fight-or-flight effects);
* Positive self-talk is needed – this has to be carried

out in the past, present and future tense;
* Stop pushing others away – give positives to others
and hear positives from them;
* Self-talk is an area to develop so that's where we
go next.

> Reena: Summary agreed. Trying to recall individual
> memories to self-talk is hard; I've obviously filed
> them deep.

Zuby: I'm beginning to see how difficult this is but I
can also see you are part of the group of survivors
that goes on to be successful and happy. Believe in
yourself. I read an excellent book – made me feel
we're on the right lines in dealing with the situation.

> Reena: How fast do you read?! And what book?

Zuby: Like I said, we'll make progress. Here's a
couple of questions; the book says a listener (me)
should ask:
"What problems, if any, do YOU think the abuse
has left you with?"
"What are the main things YOU would welcome
help with now?"

> Reena: I'll think it through. But going down this
> route tomorrow won't be nice.

Zuby: You don't have to and I won't take any
offence or negativity if you change your mind. I'm
in this till the end or until you tell me otherwise.
The book says people are often let down by the

professionals who fail to ask the right questions and then dismiss individuals who don't talk, even though the individual really does not know what to offer and what not to offer.

> Reena: That makes sense.

Zuby: It says survivors often just need to be asked the right questions by someone who is willing to listen, willing to give you time. It says people want to talk but aren't given the opportunity and are obviously uneasy about offering the information due to blame/shame. This is what you have said before. So I am humbled that you have shared this with me and I won't let you down. It also says that if you see someone express emotion, it might give you affirmation that you were treated badly – so I don't feel so bad about last week. I will try and be better though.

> Reena: I'm not sure 'want to talk' is the exact phrase, can't think what is, though; it's a strange one.

Zuby: Many survivors, for reasons already discussed, find it very difficult to raise or discuss their own history of abuse. This does not mean that survivors do not want to be asked or to be offered an encouraging atmosphere for disclosure. Indeed, many have been sending out signals since their childhood in an occasionally desperate hope that these will be picked up and acted on. If professionals keep waiting for clients to be ready they may wait forever. 'I'm a survivor. I want acknowledgement, receptivity and understanding. I just want someone to sit over there and listen to me…I need my story to be witnessed, and that's the validation I'm looking for.'[2]

> Reena: But I hate that you know? *I hate that someone knows 🤢.

Zuby: That's because you feel they'll judge.

> Reena: Yes.

Zuby: But I haven't and I won't because I have read around this and understand that the perpetrator is at fault.

> Reena: Thank you. Can I ask something?

Zuby: Of course.

> Reena: You said you built up to being able to look me in the eye and then give me a hug. Is the reason you couldn't do these initially because you didn't want to associate with me?

Zuby: I read that counsellors shouldn't show emotion because you might think they're judging you. You got it wrong; it didn't cross my mind that I shouldn't associate with you… I was afraid I'd get upset.

> Reena: OK, thank you.

Zuby: You know, of course, none of these things should have happened to you. You were not at fault in even the tiniest way. Fault is with the absolute *£@#*@. You did brilliantly and you took control.

> Reena: Thank you.

Day Nineteen

As we walked, there were times that she behaved like a child – she had uncontrolled frustration and tears, but we talked until she was able to continue calmly with the discussion.

Zuby: So what did you get out of our walk?

> Reena: Pinpointing exactly how I can change the language to rewire my brain successfully, you literally being there for me and not running when the going gets tough (I wouldn't blame you if you had), and giving just the right amount of push without it being too much.

Zuby: I've read it is good to share a little so that you can see that the listener's reaction reflects the horror of your experience. Anyone would react similarly – again, hopefully validating the fact that you weren't to blame and that the perpetrator was an unbelievably horrible individual.

> Reena: Read and heard but just don't know what to respond.

Zuby: Just say you know you don't need to feel ashamed, you're not to blame and you were never at fault.

Reena: It wasn't my fault, I didn't get myself into the situation but I did get myself out.

Zuby: You sound positive now, which is good, but you went back to that child and struggled to get the words out. But you did do it.

Reena: I didn't realise I went back to that but I did struggle to say it out loud x

Zuby: Next steps: rewrite using the correct language. Then you'll be able to say it more easily. And you might actually believe it.

Reena: Telling you was cr*ppy, going through memories to rewire was cr*ppy and going back there to rewire will be the same, but I know it's all for good reason. Sorry to ask, you don't have to answer. Was your dad ever on liquid morphine?

Zuby: He was. He had a drip with a button attached with which he could activate a dose when he needed.

Reena: Dad's been on it for a week; I had no idea 😞

Zuby: My dad got better. There's hope.

> Reena: Thank you, Zuby. Dad can leave hospital in the next couple of days :). Here's the A3.

Zuby: I know I didn't react well before but I'm not sure you should sanitise it quite so much. Use the positives to counter the horrible parts rather than remove them altogether.

> Reena: I'll look at it again and resend.

Zuby: He had no right to control you – full stop. If there is anything else – and I hope there isn't – but if you need to say anything, I can deal with it. I can't always help my physical reaction, but I can deal with it. I'm seeing this through.

> Reena: There are details but they are details that don't need to be dug up. I've picked out a range that covers most things.

Zuby: Just include what you did before. Those events clearly were significant enough for you to note down so don't remove them. Write exactly what you showed me, but turn it round so that you have none of the responsibility for any of his actions. Do you see?

> Reena: I was terrified of him and of not agreeing and 'falling in line'.

Zuby: You'd been trained but the reason you didn't say what you wanted was because he had told you what would happen if you did. He threatened you and you were scared. Is that correct?

Reena: Yes.

Zuby: 1) He had no right to control you, to choose your friends, phone and clothes. He was wrong! 2) He had no right to... He was wrong to get drunk, violent and abusive. He was criminal, wicked and evil to act in the way he did. He frightened you to death. Years later you shake as you fight to get the words out to talk about what happened to you, you're traumatised and it's having an impact on your mental and physical health. It's true he did not have the right to do any of those things but, additionally, he was plain wrong – a criminal. He was despicable, selfish, egotistical, controlling, wicked, sadistic and manipulative. How could you in any of your younger years have done anything differently in that reality? He used a stun gun on you and tried to strangle you. He abused you. He had no right. I can't think of a child behaving in any other way. You were in survival mode; you still are to some extent. That is why you must not feel shame, blame or anything negative. You got away, you rebuilt your life and you are taking back control. I'm sorry if I've gone too far.

Reena: Your words are powerful and reading them over helps, so thank you.

Zuby: Focus on the great afternoon you're about to have. Go make a difference. A life worth living.

Day Twenty

Reena: Dad's home 😆

Zuby: At your grandparents'?

Reena: Yes, at their house, but it's so much better x
He's sleeping now. I'm getting him some bits from
home that he's requested.

Zuby: I still think you have a food issue.

Reena: Of all the issues, food is not one. No, it was
nice; I enjoy flavoursome food 😊

Reena: A good day 😊 Dad is not in hospital. I feel
OK staying here :)

Zuby: Tomorrow I'll be listening out for your
positive talk towards others.

Reena: That means I have to talk to others!

Zuby: And you accept any positives that come your
way. Just don't bite anyone's head off. We'll take it
from there.

Reena: Right, here's my next one – I've updated it.

Zuby: This is more honest and attaches the blame
squarely where it belongs. But now you've lost the
parts where you recognise that you were not at fault.
Add that and then I think you're there. Make sense?

Reena: Yes.

Zuby: He is a monster.

Reena: Agreed.

Zuby: The written word here is so unlike anything you write in its formality and structure and grammar. It doesn't sound like you. This is what I meant the other day when I said you go back to sounding like a child. Not being picky, I think it's relevant and worth reflecting on. It's not a criticism.

Reena: I could have easily effed and blinded throughout but I didn't want that to detract from what was being said.

Zuby: I will say something in a minute. It just shocks me and then I don't know what to say.

Reena: I don't like shocking you x

Zuby: I think even a little bit of extra detail creates an awful graphic. I'm so, so sorry you had to live this. How do you feel, now you have this in writing?

Reena: 1) Extra careful where I leave my diary, and 2) I keep reading over it, I'm not sure yet.

Zuby: Do you think you could read it to another person?

Reena: On a good day, yes.

Zuby: What an evil, sadistic individual!

Reena: Yes, Zuby.

Zuby: How will it help you?

Reena: I can go back to it, read it and read certain parts over again and make any notes on it?

Zuby: But the important part, relating to rewiring, is that you can see what an animal he was, that he was to blame and that you were not.

Reena: And seeing it and hearing it again and again will do that.

Zuby: So you can admit to yourself that you weren't in control.

Reena: Yes.

Zuby: So it wasn't your fault. So you mustn't feel ashamed, dirty or think of yourself in a negative or derogatory manner.

Reena: The fault and the comment after that are separate.

Zuby: You must not use the words he used against you to control you. Oh Reena, if you can agree and know it wasn't your fault you can see what a 💩 he was; how is it possible that you still feel shame? To rewire you must say it.

Reena: I'll do tomorrow x

Zuby: Can't you say those words? You believe it wasn't your fault?

Reena: Yes, I can just about do that now. Shame? Dirty? Damaged? Etc?

Zuby: Can you say you are not the above? The first step is to say it, then to repeat it and then you will believe it. Pls say it.

Reena: Not out loud; I don't like the words.

Zuby: There's no one with you? No one will hear except you. Txt me a sentence with those words in the negative. Please, begin the rewiring.

Reena: I shouldn't be ashamed?

Zuby: Yes. But a statement, not a question.

Reena: I shouldn't be ashamed.

Zuby: Say: —'I am not... I have nothing to be...'

Reena: I have nothing to be ashamed of.

Zuby: Because it wasn't your fault. Well done. Tomorrow you can add that to your notes. Connect the no fault–no control–no shame. Are you alright?

A moment or two passes...
That's a no then.

> Reena: A lot of the shame and that group of words relate to the fact that I was 13 and moving in with him young, etc. I've felt somewhat stupid about the physical attacks, but that's going as I'm ridding myself of the blame.

Zuby: You were 13. Your mum kicked you out; he pretended he cared as part of the grooming. Right?

> Reena: Yes, all facts.

Zuby: So do you see that the no fault–no shame is linked? Imagine a girl of 13 (not you), who did what you did in the same circumstances – would you think she was to blame, should be ashamed?

> Reena: Mildly. The shame and feeling grubby is hard to explain. It's not about the blame. Don't worry about it; I'll sort it.

Zuby: I don't understand how you can believe that you weren't to blame and yet you feel ashamed. How? Try to answer this: Would you tell that girl she should be ashamed?

> Reena: I understand that I wasn't to blame, that I wasn't in control, but I feel d*rty and grubby that it happened, like it's a d*rty little secret. Like I'll always be tarnished because of it. No, I wouldn't.

Zuby: Right, so tell yourself that, too. It can't be undone, but you can take control of how you feel about it as an adult even if you felt dirty then – now you understand the circumstances, you can change how you feel. You don't need to judge yourself, just like you wouldn't judge a 13-yr-old standing before you. He told you it had to be a secret for his benefit. Now you can rewire. We can try again tomorrow. So you have made progress tonight. You have nothing to be ashamed of. You're not dirty. You are an intelligent, professional individual.

Day Twenty-one

As the working day was coming to an end, Reena passed by the window of my office in a hurry. I followed to check she was alright and saw she was holding back tears. I gave a little reassuring smile and asked if she would like to talk. We met up for a coffee and she told me that, as the working day was ending, her self-hate was rising to unmanageable levels. I listened to how she described herself as undeserving of good things and feeling almost more comfortable with bad days. She managed the tears and went home. The texts began later that evening.

> Reena: I just wanted to thank you for everything, Zuby. For really listening, for wanting to help and for giving me so much of your precious time; please know that I really do appreciate it. I'm really taken aback by your caring nature and your genuine interest to help. I am sorry that I've somewhat exposed you to something that you didn't necessarily have to think about or deal with beforehand. I know I have my low days and times but you have really

given me a different outlook on everything and I know that I won't live in the fallout of it all forever x

Zuby: Just want to help and please don't apologise. You deserve to reach your dreams and not be stopped by the past.

Reena: Questions, please.

Zuby: Who is the real you? Apparently, people who have been through trauma create a false self. They create a person that they think will be liked and they suppress their real self (this relates to what you said about not wanting to lose yourself).

Reena: I have no idea!! I was timid and quiet in the situation and then built a front.

Zuby: 🥺 Give it some thought. You said you didn't want to lose the real you, and yet in their bid to survive, people create a persona to be liked. Who are you really? You can be the person you want to be.

Reena: I think I'm kind-hearted and hard-working.

Zuby: What I'm getting at is this – it is time to do away with the front you sometimes feel you have to put on. It takes a lot of energy. Be that kind-hearted person. You are hard-working and you don't hide that. You can trust a little, especially at work. Give positives and accept them, too (self-compassion). Can you start to do that?

Reena: Yes. I won't get it right all of the time though, not at first. I don't want to lose my 'confidence' though, even if a lot of it is a front.

Zuby: You keep the parts that are you and lose the parts that you developed to survive.

Reena: I'll have to differentiate between them first; they've been a habit for a long time now.

Zuby: Exactly, that's what I'm asking you to do. Well, this is the self-compassion I spoke of. Allow yourself to be you and believe that people will still accept and like you. The self-compassion means that you will allow yourself to not feel ashamed or dirty, etc, because you won't blame yourself for any of the things that happened. Then you will accept who you are. Making any sense?

Reena: 👍

Zuby: When there is physical violence, it is easier to see who is to blame because the perpetrator physically harms the victim (leaves bruises, etc). A person will still feel traumatised, still feel blame.

Reena: The shame and disgust is not from the physical violence.

Zuby: When the abuse is of a sexual nature the victim feels that shame because they feel they 'allowed' it to happen. Didn't fight back, etc. The feeling of being dirty remains for longer. I wanted to say this before but the topic is of such a personal nature, I couldn't.

Reena: Understandable.

Zuby: Could this be the reason?

Reena: ☝ That's it.

Zuby: I don't think any less of you, nor do I think you should be ashamed or feel dirty. The sexual abuse and the physical abuse were both equally wrong and you could stop neither. Is this getting closer to explaining your feelings?

Reena: Yes.

Zuby: You don't need to be embarrassed or ashamed. You weren't at fault. No one deserves to be abused, no matter what they have done. So whatever you feel you did, it did not warrant what he did to you.

Reena: I can agree that I wasn't at fault but I can't shift the feeling of shame, d*rty and disgust that it happened.

Zuby: First you must accept that even that part was not your fault even if you, at first, willingly moved in with him.

Reena: I'm struggling with the fact that the blame and disgust are not linked ☹

Zuby: If you feel disgust it's because deep down you think you were complicit.

Reena: Makes sense.

Zuby: You think you somehow deserved it. But you didn't. He 'taught' you to think you did, then all those around you demonstrated disgust and blame towards you, so that is what you have come to believe.

Reena: Arghh, I wish I could explain it better. The physical violence I don't feel disgusted or d*rty from. It's the fact that what happened from a young age I hate, that's where I feel d*rty and disgusting.

Zuby: I understand that.

Reena: I feel d*rty that it happened TO me, I can accept that I wasn't to blame for it (need a hair pulling out emoji).

Zuby: This is the same emotion as many abused children feel. One reason is that they have a reaction to the sexual abuse that they don't want. Do you understand what I'm saying? I'm sorry it's so personal.

Reena: I've read it myself; I know what you mean.

Zuby: Could that be the reason you feel this way?

Reena: Maybe, there's something more/different, though – just the fact that it did happen.

Zuby: What could that be? Explain your feelings, maybe I can pick it out.

Reena: It's literally that, the fact that it did happen, that it took place.

Zuby: The fact that it happened to anyone of that age, committed by anyone of his age, means the child involved has no control. You have to see that you had no control.

Reena: Agreed, but it's disgusting and it happened to me (without meaning to sound like a victim) and that makes me disgusting.

Zuby: Would you think a child who had been through a similar experience was disgusting?

Reena: No, I wouldn't; but I do 😔

Zuby: Then linger on that thought. You wouldn't think she was disgusting. So show yourself some compassion, too.

Reena: And no one else would think that of her but I'd bet she'd feel it herself.

Zuby: You should be disgusted in him. He was dirty and disgusting. That child would be wrong to feel that, wouldn't she? What would you say to her?

Reena: I wouldn't, I'd just hold her and let her get cross.

Zuby: And after that… to help her recover for the future, what would you tell her?

Reena: I honestly don't know. Say she couldn't let him win; she had to show him he hadn't won.

Zuby: He did it first, then your mum, the safeguarding people, the courts and then your friends. They all told you the wrong thing. They used that language when referring to you but it was they who were wrong. You associate disgust with yourself because of the messages society gave you. Now society has changed. There are new messages out there. They all say the same thing. The girl did nothing wrong and she is not dirty. She's a human being who was trapped by a monster and couldn't have done anything differently. You couldn't have done anything differently. You were forced into this. You are a kind-hearted, hard-working individual. Do you think you can write these messages down in your notes? The rewiring around this feeling must begin, too.

Reena: Oh my word. If I was talking to that 13-year-old girl then I would want to grab her by the shoulders and shake her until she agreed so I can see how frustrating it must be for you.

Zuby: I'm not frustrated at all. I'm just willing this conversation to lead to an answer.

> Reena: But it won't lead to the answer you want :(

Zuby: I'm desperate to find an answer for you. Not today, but can't we start that rewiring? Don't give up on yourself. Please.

Zuby: Self-talk is the answer but will of course take time.

Zuby: First, we have to accept that you feel disgust toward yourself and then make the intention to remove any thoughts of self-loathing. Accept the feelings are wrong even if you feel that way. Understand the reasons you feel this way (what he did, what he said, how others reinforced his views, how society reinforced his views and how we now acknowledge the bias in society when it comes to sexual abuse). Then every time your thoughts come to the fore, you immediately use positive self-talk (include evidence from above) to counter them. Your self-talk is something like this: 'He is the disgusting one, he could have stopped but chose not to; I wasn't in control, I wasn't to blame'.

Zuby: Go through this sequence every time those feelings of disgust arise, until the positive self-talk becomes second nature. Then you will start to believe it.

> Reena: Do you think it will really become second nature?

Zuby: No doubt. That's what survivors say.

Reena: This process is going to be hard to accomplish.

Zuby: It will always be part of your history but you'll be able to live with it because through this process you will learn to live with it.

Reena: Because I completely believe the current emotions and they're very securely attached.

Zuby: They're hard-wired hence the need for repetition. That bit is actually quite factual. It's the things he said, they said.

Reena: I genuinely feel that they're much more personal than that (I'm not trying to be argumentative). I don't feel it.

Zuby: You feel what you have been hard-wired to feel.

Reena: Sorry, I'm not trying to be awkward. I'm willing you to be right and to really agree and feel that way but I can't lie and say I do.

Zuby: First, acknowledge how you feel. Say it. You've said it before, you can state how you feel.

Reena: I feel disgusting, d*rty and grubby.

Zuby: Why do you use an *?

Reena: I can't do that word.

Zuby: But step 1 is to acknowledge how you feel, factually. You say that word in your head, don't you?

> Reena: I kind of mime/whisper it.

Zuby: So you use it.

> Reena: Yes, it's my vocab but I don't like that one. Can say the other 2 OK.

Zuby: I understand, but to start the rewiring you must first have a starting point from which you will move forward. Is it a word he used?

> Reena: Yes.

Zuby: Acknowledge how you feel.

> Reena: I'll type it but I'm not saying it.

Zuby: Typing is fine.

> Reena: I feel disgusting and I feel dirty because of what happened.

Zuby: Next, tell yourself that you shouldn't feel that way.

> Reena: I am not disgusting and dirty because what happened was not my fault. What happened is disgusting but I am not.

Zuby: Next, write down what others did or said that wired you to believe this.

> Reena: Mum, teachers and friends shunned me and were derogatory towards me. SS has the same attitude and 'OK'ed it' by their response/lack of. He never put himself in a position of blame and was derogatory towards me. When I did grow to try and stand up for myself I was met with the response "No one forced you to stay" 😠.

Zuby: How were they derogatory? What language did they use?

> Reena: An overall change in attitude towards me.

Zuby: It will relate to how you feel now. They said something to you – what was that?

> Reena: I remember that there was a male teacher who worked in the design department (which was where I spent most of my time) and he'd been asked and told to make sure that he was in a union 😬 And if my uniform wasn't 110% or I'd forgotten some stationery, there were snide comments of "Wasn't like that in Year 9" or "I'm not exactly surprised" and "That says it all". It was much about their sudden change in demeanour.

Zuby: So that made you feel at fault. There will be language they will have used, too, that you're not saying or you don't recall. You stated another term he used towards you in your notes on Sunday.

Reena: He did, yes; he used all sorts.

Zuby: That's what I meant. That language, derogatory language, is what makes you believe them. So that language you have equated to dirty, disgusting. Right?

Reena: OK.

Zuby: Do you agree?

Reena: I want to.

Zuby: Do you think that suggestion makes sense?

Reena: Probably, to someone wired properly.

Zuby: Right. So now you know (but don't believe) why you talk about yourself in those derogatory ways.

Reena: Getting there.

Zuby: Next, whenever those thoughts, feelings and language come to you, you must counter them with positive self-talk (although you won't believe the positive self-talk).

Reena: Mind if we stop for tonight after I've answered this one? Sorry, getting hard.

Zuby: Of course. I'm sorry.

Reena: He's the disgusting one who did disgusting things. He could have stopped himself but chose not to. I was not to blame; I am kind-hearted, hard-working and a good person. I am a good granddaughter and daughter. I am a loyal friend.

Zuby: You did it! First time is the hardest. You did it. Well done! I'm here if you need me. Remember that.

It had taken numerous texts to 1.51 am to reach that point – it was exhilarating because it was the first time she had even been able to utter those words. The next day we were full of positivity; we couldn't wait to get the conversation going again that evening.

Day Twenty-two
Zuby: Let's start from the positives of today: acknowledge that you have moved forward on the blame aspect of the physical abuse. Can you acknowledge that?

Reena: Yes.

Zuby: If you can progress in one area, you can in the other.

Reena: Yes, but if I throw the towel in this will be where it is.

Zuby: First, accept the feelings you have are wrong (but that you do feel that way).

Reena: See, we're at a hurdle already.

Zuby: Tell me how you feel.

Reena: You know how I feel, Zuby.

Zuby: I want you to acknowledge it – step 1.

Reena: Disgusting, d*rty, ashamed, repulsive. Shall I go on?

Zuby: If you want to acknowledge and accept how you feel, yes.

Reena: Side note: if I sound sharp via text then I apologise in advance. I hate this part and therefore I go into defensive mode – I'll try not to.

Zuby: Again, no need to apologise. You are defensive because it's painful and you may also feel you don't deserve the time so push people away. But I'm not going away.

Reena: Disgusting, dirty, revolting, loathsome, repulsive.

Zuby: Now say that you don't need to feel that way even though you don't believe it.

Reena: How can I say something I don't believe?

Zuby: Because it will help you to rewire.

Reena: I don't need to feel disgusting, revolting, dirty, repulsive and loathsome.

Zuby: 'I shouldn't...'

Reena: Zuby, I can't do this.

Zuby: Please.

Zuby: I know you are not disgusting, dirty, loathsome or repulsive. I believe it with a passion. Trust me. Now you say it.

Reena: I'm not dirty, disgusting, loathsome, revolting or repulsive. I feel sick lying.

Zuby: That little girl, if she said she felt what you feel, how would you tackle that?

Reena: I have no idea because I've yet to find something that works for this part.

Zuby: I'm not asking you to find something that works. Take a step back. A girl is standing in front of you. She says she feels dirty and disgusting. What are you going to say to her in that moment?

Reena: I'd say 'Talk to me'; I'd tell her I was there and I wasn't going anywhere; I'd tell her I'm on her side and will fight with her. I'd let her know it's OK to be upset and to get cross and that I'll stay with her.

Zuby: She spoke to you; she was full of self-loathing.

Reena: So I'd be full of compassion, of nurture, of care.

Zuby: Yes, you would. What are the words you'd say to her?

Reena: It's easier when it's a child. You can't do that with a 25-year-old (DON'T).

Zuby: Then start with the child. She's spoken to you; she's waiting for your response.

Reena: I'd ask why; I'd tell her all the different ways she was wonderful and ask how someone who was all of those things could feel that way. I've said I would (but please don't do that to me).

Zuby: I know but you need to hear it.

Reena: I'll end up arguing back with evidence of why I'm not and it won't end well.

Zuby: You can argue all you like; I won't be deterred from telling the truth.

Reena: There's no way that I can sit and accept them so I'll give a counterpoint.

Zuby: Feel free to counter, that's what I expect, but I will counter-counter.

Zuby: You said honestly what you feel about yourself. Now begin to understand the reasons you feel this way (what he did, what he said, how others reinforced his views, how society reinforced his views and now acknowledge the bias in society when it comes to sexual abuse). You're a good person, talented and dedicated.

> Reena: I don't believe any of this.

Zuby: Wow, you're in a rotten, stubborn mood!

Silence.

Zuby: But I'm not giving up because I know you deserve more. He taught you – told you – you should feel this way, didn't he?

> Reena: Compliments genuinely bring out the worst in me. You think I'm being negative by being sarcastic with people... I'm doing them a favour. It's ingrained and, more than that, it's genuinely my own belief now.

Zuby: I know and we're trying to change that, aren't we?

> Reena: 👍

Zuby: The language he used makes you feel the way you do – he did that to you. Yes?

> Reena: Yes, but I agree with him.

Zuby: Because he told you, then the social services, etc, affirmed his words with their actions – yes?

Reena: And the teachers, my mother and sister.

Zuby: Correct – so they all wired you to believe the negative view.

Reena: It will take a brain surgeon to unwire that.

Zuby: So now, can you accept the way you feel has a lot to do with the way others shaped you – yes/no?

Reena: A lot to do with it, yes. But I don't feel this way entirely because of them, I feel this way because of what happened and what happened was x, y and z so therefore I am x, y and z. I know you're pulling your hair out, I'm sorry.

Zuby: I understand that. I will move onto that but at this stage I just want you to learn the language.

Reena: I dare say that you've done all the fixing that can be done.

Zuby: It's like reading. First learn to decode then comprehend. Didn't you make progress in the other areas we've been talking about?

Reena: Yes, but this one's stubborn.

Zuby: I know, but we can do the same here, too, in time. Pls believe me.

Silence…

Zuby: When we started you felt the same about the physical abuse. Now you have moved forward. There are 2 reasons you feel the way you do: 1) what people said to you, people important to you and society generally.

                       Reena: I didn't feel this strongly.

Zuby: 2) because you think you should have somehow stopped the sexual abuse yourself.

          Reena: And that the abuse was all the words I've used and that abuse happened to me so that makes me all of those words.

Zuby: It was done to you. It might have been all of those words because he made it so. Sex is a normal, healthy part of life. He has made you feel it's disgusting because you didn't consent. Under 16, it is statutory rape even if a child says they wanted to. A child is not capable in the law's eyes of making such a decision.

              Reena: Reading, can't reply. Feel sick 🤢.

Zuby: Me, too. But I have to state the facts to try and make you see. You were forced into acts you couldn't have consented to. Additionally, you couldn't scream out, call for help because he hurt you. You had to survive. Your mind and body dealt with this the way it could to survive (freeze).

Further silence...

Zuby: Return the dirty, disgusting, loathing language to him. He is those things; not you. Is this making any sense?

> Reena: Yes.

Zuby: I believe you when you tell me how you feel.

> Reena: Please don't ask me to go back and self-talk these parts. I absolutely can't.

Zuby: OK, but I want you to do the following because the evidence is that this will work, in time:
1) Acknowledge how you feel (you have done this).

> Reena: My chest is tight all across and my entire torso is knotted; this is too hard, Zuby 😖

Zuby: 2) Tackle that belief by accepting others wired you to use those words (him, SS, peers, teachers, your mum and society). Learn the facts, even though you don't believe them. Just know them. I'm sorry it's so difficult.

> Reena: Don't be sorry, you're willing it to work and you're really not giving up. You're amazing, Zuby, you really are; it's just really, really hard. Go slowly.

Zuby: 3) Then every time your thoughts come to the fore, you immediately use positive self-talk (include evidence from above) to counter them.

Reena: Understood.

Zuby: Self-talk can relate to your feelings instead of the actions if the actions are too painful to recall.

Reena: 

Zuby: Your self-talk is something like this: 'He is the disgusting one, he could have stopped but chose not to; I wasn't in control, I wasn't to blame. I am kind-hearted and hard-working. I am a fantastic daughter, friend (go on for as long as you like).
Silence…

Zuby: You say it again and again and again. I know you won't believe it, but do it because the evidence does show it will rewire you. In the end you will believe it, I promise.

Reena: He is the repulsive one, he could have chosen to do the right thing but he never did; I wasn't in control and it wasn't my fault. I'm a good person, a loving daughter and granddaughter, a loyal friend, compassionate and hard-working.

Day Twenty-three

Some evenings we watched something on TV. It was always something safe – a comedy or a wildlife documentary so that there was little chance of triggering a reaction. We would have a cup of tea and then begin to chat. I would always ask how she was feeling and it would develop from there depending on what she wanted to say. Reena told me about her life as a young child who was brought up witnessing violence between her parents. She told me that she would accompany her mother on the bus to access treatment at the hospital. When her parents finally separated, they constantly criticised the other and used her to glean information about their lives only to rubbish whatever they had been doing. She explained how she had learned how to navigate and please the parent she happened to be with on any given weekend or holiday. How she became a pleaser who met the needs of her parents, not the other way round. She was just ten years of age.

A family 'friend' began to attend garden barbeques and started to give her the attention she craved. He invited her to babysit and her mother was only too happy to get Reena out of her hair, especially now that she had a new boyfriend. He told her she was funny, interesting and mature for her age; he made her feel special by giving her time. She cried when this realisation hit her. It started so much earlier than she had thought. I explained how witnessing her parents' violent relationship had very likely made her think that violence was normal. She raised her eyebrows and said, "I actually did think that was how it was for everyone."

She explained how he had praised her and seemed to have time for her alone and each time she went to babysit, he came a little closer; from the chair to the sofa she was on and then right next to her. He began to caress and kiss her, telling her that he loved her. He told her that no one else would understand their unique love, that she wasn't a child like the others said; she was everything he wanted in a woman. Expect she wasn't a woman she was just 13 years old.

Zuby: I sincerely am sorry for making you go
through this again.

> Reena: I'm sorry I had that reaction. It's a long time
> since I've gone back to some memories and now I

remember why but you really are helping. I am OK with you knowing and I do trust you.

Zuby: So you're telling me – I'm helping you by making you shake in fear, making you cry in my office and then making you throw up in the evening? Because I feel like I'm leading you to a breakdown.

Reena: YOU are not doing any of those. It's the memories and hurt I shared which made me shake and I shared because I felt safe. I cried because I felt safe.

Zuby: Society now understands what happened to you was wrong. In law, sex with a minor is rape. There's no two ways about it. It's the law. So was it wrong that it happened to you?

Reena: I know the facts, I don't argue with the facts but the facts don't change those feelings. I'm not trying to be awkward, just honest.

Zuby: You feel guilt, too?

Reena: I'm not sure I do because I'll argue anyone down to the ground that it wasn't my fault.

Zuby: It wasn't your fault, of course. So you believe that now? Honestly?

Reena: Yes, I do now. It's fragile though, so I need to keep going with it.

Zuby: You understand you were in survival mode and there's nothing you could have done to stop him?

Reena: Yes.

Zuby: You know you were wired to believe those things because that gave him control?

Reena: Yes to the words he gave but I don't feel I was wired to believe I was disgusting, dirty, repulsive and revolting. They are genuine descriptions of how I feel about it all happening.

Zuby: You were wired to believe you were bad for his purposes. Can you accept any part of that?

Reena: No.

Zuby: Then you must think that you did have some control that you should have resisted in some way.

Reena: I am upset; I respect you and trust you and I find it hard that I can't believe what you tell me and I get frustrated with myself.

Zuby: Maybe the screen is getting in the way. I can't judge what's happening during the pauses.

Reena: The screen allows the honest, frank conversations to happen. They're rubbish conversations to have, I'm going to get upset. We can try f2f.

Day Twenty-four

So we met up the next day, after work. We knew it wasn't going to be pleasant. I always had a knot in my stomach but also determination. I had read hours of research and testimonies and I was desperate to find answers for her. I hoped she would say something that would lead to a connection and a solution. She told me how she had been allowed to go out for the whole day on a Saturday to 'see friends'. She would take a bus to town in the morning and that's the last her mum and stepdad would see or hear of her until early evening. They never contacted her to see if she was alright or when she would be home or even if she might need a lift home. Unsupervised, feeling unloved and somewhat in the way, she spent the day with him. He would pick her up from town and envelope her in attention. He told her he loved her, wanted to be with her and that he had all the time in the world for her. He said that the mother of his child didn't understand him like she did. She was the most special person in his life. He would then take her to dirty, little hotel rooms for sex and then gently remind her not to tell anyone or she would be the one in trouble. Reena told me how stupid she felt to have believed him and how confused she was at the time; if it was all **OK** why couldn't she share it with her parents? Anyway, she explained, they were never there to talk to.

Zuby: You're such a brave person, Reena. You did
so well today with such difficult conversations.

> Reena: Thank you for today, Zuby. Everything you
> say makes sense and I know it's because of all the
> time you put into reading up on everything. I do
> want to get there and I am trying. I'm sure I must
> be incredibly frustrating sometimes and I do really
> appreciate your patience.

Zuby: Whatever judgements society makes, it changes nothing. The truth remains the truth. These feelings are typical of ACEs. Try this to fix them…
Shame and self-hatred:

- Acknowledge how you feel – your feelings are real. But they are not justified. Self-talk, e.g.: I am a good person. I know this because of how others talk to me and interact with me (accept compliments).
- I am kind. I helped… by…
- I make a positive difference to the lives of others (think of someone you have helped that day).
- I love myself because of the difference I make to others.

> Reena: I struggle to explain it and this was fairly close: It involves feeling unworthy of respect or positive consideration by others, feeling like you deserve to be judged and criticised and feeling embarrassed in front of others. A person may feel that, because they've had such experiences, something about their very being (as a person, not just a sexual being) has been permanently tainted in a way that decreases their value and how anyone who knows about it would see them.

Zuby: I have gone from knowing nothing about you to knowing everything you have shared. You are worthy of being a friend, worthy of praise regarding everything you do.
Self-destructive behaviour/irritability:

- Acknowledge your feelings; they are real. It is OK to be angry but be angry at the causes, not at others. You can try and push people away because you think you are not worthy of positive attention, praise or even time but you are wrong. Self-talk e.g.: (deep breath), people are interested in me because I have something to give and something valuable to say.

- That compliment is accurate – I am good at...

> Reena: Thank you for your messages x I'll read through them shortly.

She added to her A3 sheet and sent it to me.

Zuby: So, you did the first part – acknowledged your feelings and stated it was wrong for you to feel that way. You haven't yet written why you feel that way (the actions of various people). Use the correct terms, even though I know you don't like them – (statutory) rape. That's what it was.

> Reena: They aren't quick fixes.

Zuby: I know – that's why I ask. Notice you missed them out. I'm ready for a pause; take your time.

> Reena: I'm getting wound up and cross now – partly this, but mostly a delayed reaction from our conversation 😖

Zuby: This is the time to use those breathing exercises. You are safe in this moment.

> Reena: Breathing.

Zuby: Make sure you're calm. Take your time to make that happen. You've dealt well with the present. Now let's deal with the past.

> Reena: Former victims of child abuse are typically changed by the experience, not only because they were traumatised but because they feel a loss of innocence and dignity and they carry forward a heavy burden of shame. Emotional, physical and sexual child abuse can so overwhelm a victim with shame that it actually comes to define the person, keeping her from her full potential.

Zuby: I've read that one. Others say it didn't keep them from their potential.

> Reena: I pick out bits from them that sound accurate and which I can identify with.

Zuby: You started to trawl the Internet for articles that reinforce how you currently feel. Look at the very many articles that are full of hope.

Silence…

Zuby: Please end the day on a positive. You did really well today. You made progress. You really did. Make sure you tell yourself and that you believe it.

> Reena: Yes.

Zuby: You have your whole life in front of you. You will be defined by your achievements to date and to

come, not by the past. Make that commitment to
yourself. You deserve it.

> Reena: Thank you. You praise and congratulate
> me but your levels of patience, willing and
> determination are astonishing x

Day Twenty-five

As the boss, I proposed a new procedure for staff to text me at 7.00
am if they were unable to attend work that day and, for the first
time ever, she did just that.

> Reena: I'm not sure if I'll be in in the morning. I am
> OK, Dad is OK. I will text properly shortly when I
> have sorted things x I promise I am OK x x

Zuby: I need to know what's happened, pls.

> Reena: I'm OK. He came to the house moments
> after Uncle Steven had left so I thought it was Uncle
> Steven coming back but it wasn't and he got me.
> I had my alarm and I got away but not before he
> threw me around a bit. The neighbours phoned
> 999 and I've spoken to the police. I'm staying at
> Grandma and Granddad's tonight. Zuby, I promise
> I am OK – sore and bruised, but not my face – I
> am OK. I will come and see you whenever is best
> tomorrow but I'm going to be tender so can't focus
> on work.

Zuby: Has he got away?

Reena: At the moment. He was in his car so they're looking for that.

Zuby: Where do you live? I'm going to go look for his bloody car.

No answer.

Zuby: Does he have that private no. plate?

Reena: Yes.

A small pause…

Reena: No. Stay at home and hold your boys extra tight.

Zuby: We have an empty house on Brakeford Road. If you don't want to stay at someone else's house, you can stay there and have your independence.

Reena: Thank you, Zuby. I don't know what to say x I wasn't going to tell you this but you have shared more tears with me and given me more support in these past few weeks than my mother ever did.

Zuby: Her loss entirely. You're a fabulous, good person. You'll achieve much. You're still functioning on the cortisol and adrenalin. But you will then experience the real emotions once those coping hormones have lessened. You can prepare for that now.

> Reena: Positive self-talk?

Zuby: You're going to think about what might have happened, you'll catastrophise. That's where you have to stop your thoughts and focus on positives.

> Reena: I like this emotionless state but I'm wary.

Zuby: You know that's temporary. It's survival mode.

I was incensed that a person could be stalked in this way and physically attacked whilst the police were impotent and ineffective. I sent off a strongly worded e-mail to my local MP to complain, thinking that I probably wouldn't hear anything back.

Day Twenty-six

The office was busy that day but I had to take a call that came through as urgent. The MP called me back to say he, too, was appalled but that he knew the Chief of Police. He said he could help and I felt relief, so I went to find Reena to tell her the good news. It was anything but for her. She ran to the bathroom and I heard her being sick. When she came out she asked to go home and I had no choice but to let her go.

> Reena: Can you give the MP my number, please? Or revoke the request for support?

Zuby: I don't understand.

> Reena: Please, it's the thing I have control of. I know you want it to help and I understand that but I don't want him involved.

Zuby: Please don't do this.

> Reena: I don't trust them not to mess it up or get people's backs up.

Zuby: If that's what you want, then I will. Yes.

> Reena: Maybe when I'm stronger and further down the line I can ask him to support the case or something but everything is so fragile at the min I don't want a stroppy officer losing evidence or filling a form wrong or whatever they decide in order not to have to follow orders. I scared myself being how I got today; it's a long, long time since I've been like that and I didn't know it was even in me anymore.

Zuby: Then I'm sorry. I will contact the MP so you
don't need to worry about that part.

> Reena: You are trying, Zuby, and that is far more than anyone has ever done for me before, I cannot put into words how much it means. I didn't know myself that it wasn't the right thing until I had this reaction to it.

Zuby: I'm being totally honest, no dressing it up.
You have no self-compassion. I keep telling you, you
are amazing, talented, resilient, but you don't hear it
and you don't believe it.

> Reena: I appreciate and need the honesty. I shall change my positive list for positive things that I am, that I am doing. I want to fight this, I want to win.

The domestic violence support team offered their support, too, and after speaking to them on the phone, Reena had agreed to meet them at the office the next day.

> Reena: Tomorrow is feeling more and more impossible.

Zuby: It's just the DV people, not the police

> Reena: I'm broken; I'm utterly shattered. They'll want a statement and for me to press charges. I can't do that.

Zuby: You are giving up and you will lose everything you have worked for. You have finally admitted to yourself that you are a victim currently of DV.

Silence…

Zuby: You took a big step today. Can you take another to give yourself the best possible chance of ending this?

Further silence…

Zuby: This isn't going to go away by itself. Don't be a victim any longer. Let the police and DV people help.

> Reena: I hear you, I just can't take action right now; I am broken.

Zuby: Do you think by not doing anything you will fix yourself?

> Reena: I'm not even thinking about a fix right now, I've no energy for that.

Zuby: You are broken because of what he has done over the years, not because of what happened today. Place the blame with him.

> Reena: That's not what you want to hear I know, and if you want to cut me off then that's completely fine and understandable and probably makes the most sense to do.

Zuby: There are many women who escape this cycle. I will never, ever cut you off.

> Reena: You're still being nice to me after what I've put you through – stop.

Zuby: If this is going to end badly, fight, fight and fight to give yourself the best possible chance. Don't you see; you are sentencing yourself to a life of threat, pain and ultimately depriving yourself of a chance to be happy?

> Reena: I can't fight; I have no fight left. Ultimately you want me to give that statement and I'm not saying yes.

Zuby: He's going to bloody kill you and I will have to live with that forever.

Reena: This is why I want you to wash your hands
of me.

Zuby: What are you willing to do to help yourself?

Reena: I don't know that either.

Zuby: You are trapped at the bottom of a deep well.
Let someone pull you out.

Zuby: You deserve for this to end so you can achieve
your dreams.

Reena: I've reached my dream.

Zuby: You've only just started. You're not a victim.
Be a survivor.

Day Twenty-seven

I was totally perplexed by her reaction. Whereas I understood her
fear of the perpetrator and therefore the reason for not wanting to
press charges, I couldn't understand her reason for not taking the
advice of the support team. I was so concerned about her mental
well-being that I decided to visit her family home. I expected to see
her father there. I was prepared to meet the grandparents acting as
carers for her father. He would no doubt be looking weak following
his long stay in hospital and an operation for lung cancer. Once I
had shared my concern for their family member, I would be able to
walk away knowing that she was in safe hands.

I walked down the driveway and double-checked the door
number before ringing the bell. No one came to the door so I
knocked.

The door opened to a man who smiled and raised his eyebrows in anticipation of a response from me.

"Hello, I'm looking for Reena's house?"

"Yes, this is it and you are..?" he asked.

"I'm her boss. I have a few concerns about her that I wanted to share with you."

He opened the door wider and invited me in. I judged the décor and the smell of the cats as I was led through the dark hallway and into a living room. I noted the window sill lined with photographs of Reena throughout her childhood and on her graduation day.

"Tea?"

"No, thank you. I didn't expect to see you looking so well," I blurted out. He looked confused.

"I have a bit of a cough but nothing more," he said.

I explained that Reena had told me that he had been in hospital and that her work colleagues were concerned about her bruises.

"If she's back with that paedo, I'll be up there. I know where he lives!" he told me. "She's been a bit down, been walking with a friend – is that you?"

I thought it strange that he hadn't mentioned the bruise and then it occurred to me – here is a man looking healthy, who supposedly had surgery only days ago; there are no elderly grandparents to be seen and no space to put any. Perhaps *he* was the one. I bravely or foolishly asked him straight out: "Is it you? Have you been hitting her?"

He answered immediately and casually as if I had just asked him about the weather.

"No, I've never hit my children. She'll be home soon." He reached for his mobile and rang her. She picked up. He spoke to her briefly – apparently she was only five or ten minutes away. There was an uneasy silence and I felt as if I had solved the mystery. He was the culprit.

"I'll go now," I said, and "I'll catch her at work."

We both stood up for me to leave. I was relieved to be out of there as I hurried towards my car. As I crossed the road, I saw her car manoeuvring in to park at the house. We glanced at each other and she sped off. She'd been found out. I ran to my car and tried to follow her but she knew these streets well; she was long gone. I called her but she wouldn't answer. After a short time, I assumed she had stopped driving as she responded by text.

> Reena: Let them all know that they're more than entitled to be angry with me, please.

Zuby: Let's talk.

A moment's pause…

Zuby: Stop, pls.

> Reena: Nope.

Zuby: Let's talk.

> Reena: Far too messed up for that.

Zuby: Just talk to me, I'm not angry.

> Reena: That doesn't make sense.

Zuby: Please, just let's talk.

> Reena: You deserve better.

Zuby: Then talk to me.

Reena: Not worth your time.

I found where she had stopped and I pulled up behind her car. She unlocked the passenger door to let me in. She couldn't look at me.

"What is this? I stood up for you, fought for you – why? You lied to me!" To me; to her colleagues at work. To all of us.

"I told you," she sobbed, "I'm messed up."

"It was him, wasn't it? He's the one who's been hitting you?" The absence of Reena's answer was enough. She looked out of the window, not at me. "You *are* messed up, people don't do this for fun. You need help. You have a choice now; either you do exactly as I say, the doctor and the counsellors say, or you're on your own." She was clearly broken and lost but I meant it. I told her she had to find somewhere else to live, away from her dad. She agreed and we parted so that she could begin to sort her life out. We didn't text again until much later that evening.

Reena: Thank you.

Zuby: I just hope I'm not a total idiot for trying to
help you.

> Reena: I'm sorry for the past few months. By accepting your help and following it through, one day in the future you'll be able to believe me again. Driven past some rentals. Going to try and sort a Travelodge and then think about food.

Zuby: If you have finally told the truth, you still
have a job; still have your life. If there is anything
more, tell me now.

Reena: You know my dad, you know the perpetrator, you know my circumstances and you know where I need to go for help. You know everything.

Zuby: One more lie and I think that would have to be the final one.

Reena: Absolutely.

Zuby: You've caused me a lot of upset. But I've stuck with you. The grief has to stop now.

Reena: I know I have and I'll forever regret that.

Zuby: Your regret doesn't help me. Your actions here on in, will.

Reena: :) Thank you again.

Day Twenty-eight

Zuby: You can fix things by telling the truth and apologising to those you've hurt.

Reena: They won't want that tomorrow, they'll need time before they can even listen to an apology, never mind accept.

Zuby: True, but they'll want to see that they can be around you and that you can behave in a professional manner.

> Reena: People will not want to see me tomorrow plus, depending what is said at the drs in the morning, I may not be fit.

Now lacking trust, I tried to search online for the person she had named, wondering if he actually existed. I was shocked but relieved somewhat that he was named in a newspaper report dating back to when she had said it happened. It spoke of a man who, by his own admission, was too weak to resist a 16-year-old. He admitted to having a relationship with her at that age but had denied the underage charges. She had told me the truth. I sent her the article.

> Reena: First time I've seen that 😕. Never knew what his story was in the papers. 😰

Zuby: Now you know the truth.

> Reena: There were reams of messages over the years: holiday bookings, dates of hotels and evidence of moving in before 16.

Zuby: It's over – move on. I believe you in this matter. I just needed to check what you told us was true. I'm satisfied it was. You can control the present and your future. Focus on that. Focus on tomorrow. One day at a time towards rebuilding your reputation.

There was a long silence, no texts for nearly half an hour.

Zuby: Are you alright?

> Reena: We know the answer to that.

Zuby: I didn't want to, but had to have proof of the past to know that you were telling the truth. Now I have it, move on to the next truth.

Reena: What would you like next?

Zuby: Next is the drs (and anything else you think might be relevant in terms of truths that were omitted previously).

Reena: I've just tracked my entire screwed up past, genuinely don't know how I've made it this far. You can come, too, if you want to be sure I'm telling them the truth.

Zuby: Yes, I'd like to. You have made it this far; don't screw it up further. You didn't control the past – not your fault. You can control the future – your fault.

Reena: Yes. I don't know what the drs will entail tomorrow but if I've to go through my history, can you possibly hold back with any judgements until we're in the car, if that's even fair to ask?

Zuby: You've told me your history, is there something else?

Reena: There's bits, but you know the big stuff.

Zuby: What don't I know?

Reena: Not lies, just bits of history that haven't come up.

Zuby: Better to say now if it is anything that will affect trust.

Reena: DV with Mum and Dad – I defended him :/, Groomed by 13, raped at 14, loss of family members, abused until escape at 18, stalked and went to court. Decisions cost me close family who I doted on, moved back with Dad, drink made him repeat DV with me – that's it. Trying to be crystal.

Zuby: Thank you for trusting me with that. The future is for you to decide.

Reena: I need to be able to fix whatever mess I am in.

Zuby: You can.

Reena: That ship has sailed. I can give it but there's no way I should have it returned.

Zuby: It's not up to you how others decide to respond. Your mum and dad were and are inadequate parents. A child without guidance is lost and vulnerable. None of that was your fault but what you do now is absolutely in your control. Make good choices for yourself.

Reena: Yes, stop being nice.

Zuby: Where have you ended up, then? Safe or not
safe?

Reena: At Dad's at the min, he's not had a drink nor
having one. I'll be up and out early.

Zuby: Don't take the risk. You have that horrible
hotel booked, which is better than another dose of
DV.

Reena: Agreed. 'Dose of DV' – blimey, that's an
awful term!

Zuby: And knowing that your dad hits you, your
mother doesn't want to know? Have you told her he
is hitting you?

Reena: Mum won't listen to anything I have to say.
She either doesn't engage at all or shouts about
being out of order and unfair for what I did.

Zuby: So you haven't told her?

Reena: I've said it twice to her. I'm OK not having a
relationship with my mum. It never properly rebuilt
from when I was younger.

Zuby: OK, so now you have to remember you have
a job, money and independence; you don't need
anyone else to ensure your safety.

Reena: I am sorry.

Zuby: Are you really? And what for?

> Reena: For causing so much hurt, for wasting time, for making people question themselves, for causing so much upset – for everything.

Zuby: For fabricating, manipulating and exaggerating?

> Reena: For you missing your boy's bedtime, interfering with and destroying your family time.

Zuby: Probably best to talk tomorrow. Right now, after having to explain myself to the others and to have to justify your situation, not feeling too good.

Day Twenty-nine

She stayed in hotels for the next few days until I was able to help her find a more permanent place through my contacts. I helped her to settle into her new flat and we chatted as we assembled furniture. She had brought nothing with her except her work clothes.

"Did you genuinely ask him directly if it was him?" Reena asked.

"Looked him in the eye."

"Just odd that he hadn't gone out on a Saturday."

"He said he'd never hit anyone, not even when the kids were small, he said. Did he?"

"Not when I was little, no. Denies even hitting Mum. Being in that backward emotional state, when Dad started up again I needed him to be unavailable to others, he went for a lot of tests about his persistent bloody and breathless cough and I built on that, drawing on losing Andy's mum.

When I had bruises, the emotional state took another hit and I couldn't reveal the source, I had to protect him whilst providing a reason for the emotions I had – the closest I knew was my past so I used that. I am really gutted at the hurt I've caused you; I just wanted to hold you today and say 1000 times how sorry I am," Reena confessed.

"This is what I understood from this morning: current trauma, i.e. the DV situation in Feb, led to you feeling emotionally similar to the vulnerable position you were in your teens. To get recognition of how you felt, your mind made up scenarios that got you the support. Sometimes you genuinely believed your abuser had come back to hurt you again," I stated.

"I feel both dizzy and some relief. Dizzy because of everything we've tried to comprehend over a short space of time, lots of different aspects and directions, too. It often takes a few hours/days for things to fully sink in a process and there's a lot sinking in at the moment – my head feels particularly busy and a little overwhelmed. I feel relief because I have clear steps of what must be done next going forwards."

"Your mum is still around, maybe you could try and use her for support," I suggested.

"This is how I feel about her and want to say to her: 'You completely washed your hands of me, Mum. I know I was shameful and embarrassing but you completely cut me off at first, so when I was beaten up and hurt and scared I had nowhere to go, even though you were only up the road. Sending people round to scare me out did nothing other than terrify me and make his case stronger'."

"There has to be someone else," I said.

Day Thirty

Work became a challenge; people began to vie for my attention. They told me they were worried for me; that I should let Reena go. I was astounded by their lack of compassion and tried hard to reassure them that this colleague, whom we had known for years and years, was mentally ill, not evil. She needed us to help her heal but they only wanted to further dig in their heels. The texts continued.

> Reena: I'm sorry I let you down so badly and made work an impossible place for you. I'm sorry it's you that I came to with this, you that I unveiled everything to and shared the pain with. I'm sorry that it's you I've hurt. If it helps: you have really helped me to start to see that so much of what I blamed myself for was not my fault. Guided me to believe that I'm worth more than a repeat performance. Made me identify where exactly my issues are and what it is I need support with. You've reassured me and given me strength throughout this.

I let her continue without interruption.

> Reena: Now and again, this stupid illness gets too much. Too much to fight, too much to cover with a smile, too much to force energy through, and too much to pretend. I have to constantly be fighting it off for it not to take hold; when I tire, it creeps in and grabs on. And it's then, when I'm tired, that I need the most fight – to fight it off first and then carry on. And there's just no fight there. Some things can't be fixed, Zuby, no matter how wonderful, fantastic, amazing, heartfelt and genuine someone is. Some things aren't made to be fixed and that's OK x

Day Thirty-one

On our morning walk, Reena had revealed that her appointment for counselling had finally come through; she was terrified. We talked about how this would be the solution and that it would help to heal her and she seemed to take it on board, but both of us were apprehensive. We left it on a positive but as the time came closer, the negativity began to take hold. Later that evening we resumed our text conversations.

> Reena: You've helped me identify that I need help, where I need help and why I need help. You've helped me to see where things are not my fault and where I wasn't to blame. You've guided me to hand the unclean and shameful feelings over. This is more help than I've ever had.

Zuby: I'm sorry you have to go through this but I know it will help despite what they said to you at work. Prove them wrong.

> Reena: My emotions and all my fronts/barriers are going to be stripped right back and I'm going to be vulnerable and weak. But it's only then that the repairing can begin and I think we've gathered that there's a lot of damage to be repaired. I'm not far away from rock bottom as it is. I don't know if wounds will be opened and closed within the same session or if they'll be left in between sessions and I've to handle it. I am scared but I have to go through this or I'll never really be better x

Zuby: Don't feel so down. This is a step forward, please.

> Reena: I feel low because I know I'm damaged, because I know I need help, because not being repaired has contributed to me seriously hurting people who were close. Because 12 years after this started I am still an utter mess and, despite what I've achieved, that part hasn't shifted at all. I'm utterly fed up of being broken, of being weak, of needing help.

Zuby: You are stronger now; you are not that child anymore.

> Reena: That's just it; I'm not. I'm still that broken, weak, vulnerable and damaged 13-year-old.

Reena seemed so alone/estranged from those whom she needed most at this time. I couldn't quite understand why that was so I played detective again and found contact details for them. With an anxious, rapid heartbeat in anticipation of what this step could reveal, I contacted Reena's mother and sister. They sounded very concerned and not at all uncaring. They agreed immediately to meet at Reena's new flat. I was to be there, too – so that we could verify her words.

Reena unlocked the front door and I entered and, at that point, her sister and mother pulled up. She looked at me and for that split second looked furious and then resigned. We walked through the communal areas together and into Reena's flat, with only brief introductions. I explained my concerns. Reena was silent. I explained what had happened. They said they didn't blame her for any of it but that she was a rebel and it was time for her to change. I felt pleased, believing that she finally had someone close in her life that would help her through this difficult time. I explained a little more... that her dad had hit her and that, as a result, memories from the past had been triggered, that she felt inadequate and wanted to gain their love somehow; she wanted to know how.

Jan, her older sister, clearly objected to this. "You're giving her attention. She's loving this!" she declared. Her mother accused her of having 'tried it on' with her stepfather. The supportive family scenario that I had envisaged dissolved. However, her mother hugged her and said she knew it wasn't her fault and they agreed to keep in touch with Reena and thanked me for my involvement.

As they left, her mother whispered to me, "Tell Bex not to leave her partner alone with Reena." Bex was Reena's best friend. I smiled in embarrassment.

We all left the flat together, leaving Reena alone. On my way home Jan phoned to warn me to be careful, saying that her sister was a liar.

There was silence for the rest of that evening.

Day Thirty-two

> Reena: They obviously view me as some sort of nasty marriage-wrecker, being in complete control of what happened and choosing the circumstances I put myself in.

Zuby: They're in denial. They failed to protect you. Now it's too difficult for them to face their inadequacies. What they're doing is textbook. It's not you.

> Reena: That comment they made about me to you was as low as they could go. Which one said it? Mum walked you downstairs and out; was it then?

Zuby: What does it matter?

Reena: It matters. That comment is a low blow that's nothing short of nasty. I'm sorry. Please know that I AM moving forwards and I have moved a long way; I still have worries about things, it's only natural. I know I've brought them on myself, I accept that.

Zuby: I'm incredibly proud of the progress you have made in a short time. I am proud that it was me that stood by you when others didn't. The way that you've dealt with the information about your family has been like anyone would have. You're angry and hurt but you're safe and controlled. That's amazing progress and not what would have happened a few weeks ago, right?

Reena: Yes. This is what winds me up with them. They say what I did is no longer an issue, that they don't even think about it. Yet when you ask them what they want to change about me they say the lies. Agreed, there is this incident but previous to that it was when I was 13–15 where I lied about him and where I was going, etc, and that is what Jan was referring to.

Zuby: They said they are there for you. They don't blame you. Maybe they'll go away and think about it and understand better?

Reena: On the inside I'm raging. I'm raging that it happened to me, I'm raging that I was stupid enough to let it happen, I'm raging that it's still affecting me and I'm the one left picking up the pieces. I'm disappointed in myself for not being stronger, for not fighting this sooner. I've let other people down and I've let myself down; I'm weak. I want to win but I don't want to; haven't got the fight. Why me? What do I have tattooed on me that says 'Pick her, knock her down, give her sh**, she can take it'. No, she can't; she's broken, she has nothing left to give. She's all kinds of battered and bruised and she wants everything to just stop.

Zuby: You are in control now for you to define yourself in any way you choose. The biggest impact on your current life is him, the violence/sexual abuse and the beatings. The resulting fear, lack of control and shame – that's what you can't cope with today. Is that correct?

> Reena: Yes, I'm sorry, and that it's at your feet that I dump all of this.

Zuby: You have to use your energy to counter every negative thought he put there.

> Reena: I try, I really do; I promise. Maybe now you can see some of the things I'm battling. I am sorry I'm broken and it's not an easy fix. I am sorry that it's you.

Zuby: You're not broken. You are safe, in your own home, with a job. The pain of the past will go. But the pain caused by the present – you can limit now. I can limit. I forgive you for the lies; I really do understand.

> Reena: Thank you, you are wonderful. You're amazing, constantly.

In the middle of the night I received the first notification of another awful turn in how the mental illness would develop. Reena would text for help but couldn't quite control her shaking – her sentences would be incomplete. She would need to be reminded of the present and that she was safe, away from her tormentor.

> Reena: Words are broken.

Zuby: What do you mean?

> Reena: Talk, please. Now things, good things.

Zuby: I'm looking forward to seeing you at work.

> Reena: Yes.

Zuby: You will smile. You will hear laughter. You will win. This is part of the healing. Worse before it gets better. You must believe me.

> Reena: Can you stay a bit longer, please, I'm sorry to ask.

Zuby: I'm here. What shall I do? What's happened?

> Reena: I'm coming back. You need to go now. I will manage; I'm here and now and can move around now.

Zuby: What's happened?

> Reena: I know the acts were shameful and I feel awful that they happened to me and want to hide it. That's how I'd describe it now.

Zuby: Why at this time? You must sleep.

> Reena: I had a dream but it felt real, I was there again. He was on top of me. I couldn't move.

Zuby: You are safe now.

> Reena: Thank you so much. Honestly, you were really there and brought me out of it properly.

This signalled the start of nightly occurrences where Reena would say that she felt she was actually back in that situation. It was as if she was reliving the experiences. The therapist called it 're-experiencing'. In that moment, she described it as just that – she sobbed at how she felt every blow and every forced touch.

Day Thirty-three

Reena came to pick me up on her way to her doctor's appointment. She had asked me to go with her so that I could witness the truth for myself. She was crying.

"What's the matter?" I asked.

She shook her head. "Nothing." She paused. "Just worried."

At the surgery, she told the doctor the whole story – her lies, her past, her dad and her abuser.

"Am I safe to work?" she asked suddenly. The doctor finished typing up her notes and turned from the screen to face Reena. I sat quietly next to her, having been introduced as a friend. The doctor told her that that was up to her boss. She was given some medication and I felt relieved.

We went back to her flat and, as we had a cup of tea, I shared my optimism; the doctor said this medication would help. This is the beginning of the end. I cleared away a book from her sofa and flicked through the pages of her pink book – the one in which she wrote her dreams, her fears and her nightmares. I found a letter – a suicide letter to me and a list of others she was going to write to.

"So I'm spending all this time – going to the doctor, to the counsellor, explaining mental health to people at work, and all this time you were going to just give up?!" I was hurt and angry.

"I'm sorry, I wasn't going to do it. It's why I was crying in the car. I thought about it and then knew I couldn't do this, especially not to you."

We sat together and cried until we couldn't anymore. I held her hand tightly and explained that it wasn't an option and she promised me she would never go through with it, that she would call me if it ever felt like she could. There was nothing more to say so I went home, but my phone became an additional limb after that day – just in case.

> Reena: I'm sorry. I didn't think I had the strength to keep fighting. But I know now that I can have off days and it doesn't mean I've lost. I have moved the disgust from me to the acts themselves.

Zuby: Why didn't you ring the Crisis no.? Why didn't you tell me first?

> Reena: I didn't even know how I was planning to do it. I just thought that I would before long so had to write letters.

Zuby: 'You've made so much progress', I thought.

Reena: It's just got a lot harder all of a sudden.

Zuby: We both knew it would. We put everything in
place to cope.

Reena: I know and I trust you. You're honestly
helping me.

Zuby: I am trying. If you think I can't do it, if you
think I'm not doing you any good just tell me.

Reena: I'm sorry about today; that must have been
awful to read.

Zuby: After sharing, after all of our conversations.
To end like that, I couldn't deal with that.

Reena: ☹

Zuby: As the harmful present-day reactions end,
you will be left with filed memories only that you
will access and drop on your terms, without the
reaction.

Reena: Yes. Tired but accepting that disgust isn't on
me – determined. Thank you for giving me some
confirmation that what I feel is reasonable and OK.

Zuby: I want to get you to a stage where you can
just function without having to exert energy to block
out those feelings. I want you to acknowledge your
past but to know that it must not play a part in
deciding your present and future. Remember from

this morning that your anger is an asset and it will help you through. That you were put through what I can only describe as torture but that you are so strong you survived. That none of it was your fault so you must forgive yourself. You are learning to live with the past but not letting it control you now.

> Reena: I have to go on, Zuby; if I stop I don't know when I'll start again. I'm so thankful for your support. I now, more than ever, feel like, finally, I can fight this and win. With him, with the situation, I was 13 and he took that away from me, but that wasn't enough, he continued to humiliate me for a further 5 years 😢

Zuby: But not anymore. Don't let him take another second from you. Use your anger to serve you. To double your determination.

> Reena: He gets to live a life not affected at all. It's not fair.

Zuby: He's scum. People know what he did. He didn't tell the whole truth – but by his own admission – he at 37 couldn't control himself with a 16-year-old. He has no value.

> Reena: If I give in now I don't know where I'll draw the line.

Zuby: I understand you're cross about him but use that anger to fight against the harmful thoughts that he put there. Use the anger for you.

Reena: Don't read this rant if you don't want but I need to get it out: It's really not fair. I was 13; I lost all of my life from 13 to 18. I'm hurting and I'm cross and I'm upset and I'm broken and damaged and he isn't anything, he walks away and laughs. I can feel where he hurt me; I can hear his words and smell him near me. I hate him so much, him and what he did, that he chose me, that he hurt me, that he did it again and again and that it was a sport for him. I hate that he won every single time and that he can feel absolutely nothing today. He hasn't lost anything; he doesn't need to repair to feel normal. I'm still broken and I hate him for breaking me and I have to fight everyday. I hate that he's always in my head. I want to curl up and hide away from it all.

Zuby: You will do the opposite. You will fight and it will become easier. HE DOES NOT HAVE THAT HOLD OVER YOU. He cannot hurt you. He wanted you but you escaped. He never won.

Reena: Yes.

Zuby: Use that anger not to think about him but to think about you. Use that anger to re-energise. You will fight this. You are learning that time spent thinking about him is wasted. Your happiness will be created by you and not by what happens to him. He is irrelevant. He is jealous of your achievements, angry that you got away. He's a loser. Let him rot. Use the coping strategies to take your valid emotions and change them to serve you. I'm sorry no one helped you. I'm sorry you had to go through that.

I'm sorry such evil people exist. I'm sorry that you
have those feelings and memories in your head. But
you are safe now. You are in control. No one can
hurt you again.

> Reena: I want to fight it, I do.

Zuby: I want you to read your strategies. Look at
your achievements. Dream of the possibilities. Read
them until you fall asleep.

Day Thirty-four

> Reena: I can't quite tell you but I've definitely put
> an emphasis on moving forward since you hugged
> me tightly earlier. And the determination has
> only grown as the evening has gone on. I'm cross;
> I'm cross at lots of things but each time I get cross
> I say 'Sod you!' and put a little more strength and
> emphasis on what will be. There are good things
> such as your ongoing perseverance, your ability to
> always see the best in a situation, your dedication
> to always improving, your selfless soul, your loving
> nature, your commitment to ensuring people get
> what they deserve and a smile that lights up your
> face when you talk about your family. To name a
> few. Thank you for today, honestly. For working
> through the book and giving me the strength and
> confidence to move forwards.

Zuby: I can see slowly but surely you are beginning
to understand that he shaped your thoughts and

you are changing them so they are your considered,
positive thoughts and not his twisted negative ones.

> Reena: I won't give up.

Day Thirty-five

Zuby: Happy birthday: How are you feeling?

> Reena: Best not to ask because I don't want to snap
> at you.

Zuby: What is your inner voice telling you?

> Reena: Swear words.

Zuby: What is your inner voice swearing at?

> Reena: About my birthday, about me, about
> everything.

Zuby: OK, let's look at this one by one. What's it
saying about today?

> Reena: That I'm going back on all the positive
> things I said about it.

Zuby: Disarm your inner voice. Tell it your dad
hurt you so you had to leave to protect yourself, tell
it that your significant adults weren't capable of
protecting you when you needed them most – so you
had to let them know how you felt.

Reena: Yes.

Zuby: It's the first time you're challenging that inner voice, your subconscious. You must talk it down. It will get easier, I promise.

Reena: I'm so sorry. You don't deserve this. It's late; you've put time and effort into building me up. I'm sorry.

Zuby: Don't give in. You are safe, determined and you have the evidence so your rational mind will understand. You are reprogramming your brain. Changing the past indoctrination. This is how you will remove him from your present and future.

Reena: Please don't.

Zuby: I'll counter your negatives till you believe my positives.

Reena: I'm really fighting my inner voice more than ever and it's tiring, so that and having a mask for the world will be my use of energy.

Zuby: I accept what you say.

Reena: Thank you for all of your effort building up to today. I'm sorry I can't make it work instantly. I'm still committed to healing, I promise.

Zuby: You're not fighting this alone. Know that.

Reena: Today was an overwhelming plea for things to just stop for a moment, a realisation of how much energy it all takes.

Zuby: We will find a way, though. You need to hold on.

Reena: I'm holding.

Day Thirty-six

Zuby: Let me make a point – do you have any photos of your younger self?

Reena: I've found a couple.

Zuby: Hopefully you can see the innocence of that little girl. She deserved good things, didn't she? Just as you do now.

Reena: Yes, but I'm alone now. And yes, I have done that to myself, I completely accept that.

Zuby: You haven't. It was due to you being ill. You sit down, alone, and you tell yourself you are now in 2019. You tell yourself how you want to feel (all of those positives). Your body refuses to listen because it is used to reacting like it always has so you continue to feel restless, bad. You tell your body to sit still, to not react and to not move. You tell your brain how you want to think and feel from now on. Repeat several times a day. Repeat and in the end

your body will give in – it will react to your new
positive emotions because you will have rewired.

> Reena: I just don't like being whatever I am. I
> accept that I need the help and the meds but I don't
> like it.

Zuby: What 'are' you?

> Reena: We don't even know. Whatever damage or
> illness it is. I'm afraid of what they'll do. What if
> they section me?

Zuby: I know you're afraid of what your treatment
will entail but, having researched it, I'm sure it will
be talking therapy – similar to what we've done
but over a longer period of time. Not pleasant but
you're not psychotic, not hearing voices and not
dangerous so you're not going to be sectioned or
anything like that. Will be talking therapy. You will
be able to deal with it as you have done before. I'm
sure of it. After every session I'll be there to help
you carry on but I think we've come so far already
in weeks. Just think what they'll be able to do for
you.

> Reena: Yes, thank you. I so want this part of me,
> this part of my life to be done with and for good.
> I know I'm scared but, quite frankly, I'll endure
> anything just to have it dealt with and be normal for
> the rest of my life.

Day Thirty-seven

I spent a huge chunk of my day at the office fighting Reena's corner. I explained what the doctor and the counsellor had said. This was an illness just like any other; we needed to support our unwell colleague, surely? The lack of understanding and compassion came through. I was dismayed that educated people chose to display such behaviours.

> Reena: You're fighting a range of battles at work. I frustrate you no end when I can't see things from your informed, rational point of view. I'm stealing every hour from you. Just take a break from me, please.

Zuby: All of the above is wrong. Don't push me away.

> Reena: Just booking next appointments for counselling.

Zuby: From today what have you learned?

> Reena: I deserve good things.

Zuby: Blame/deserving/shame are linked. Those thoughts are wrong and have to be eradicated. You are able to do that by: positive self-talk, mindfulness, countering your inner voice and never saying anything derogatory about yourself.

> Reena: Yes.

Zuby: I've looked up all of the therapies available at Polly Hall. All say it's good to come prepared (and you really are). None of them are anything to be scared of, I promise. I've tried my best as an amateur. They'll know better.

Reena: Please know that everything you have done has helped. Mum and Jan are the easy options. I can rightfully and easily get cross at that and I can react to the people who have said the words. The hurt is from him. I hate him. I really, really hate him. I don't even want to hate him because that's too strong an emotion. It was years ago and I'm still so cross, I don't even want to not be cross because I have strength there.

Zuby: Go ahead and tell me what you learned today.

Reena: That I don't have the heart to blame that little girl because there's no way on earth it could be her fault – she needed saving but had no one to save her – that's not her fault. She survived, she assessed each situation and quickly learned the safest response She was bright, she knew what she had to do and didn't let pride get in the way of her survival. She really was groomed in every way and for much longer than originally realised. Her innocence and trusting nature was taken advantage of and used against her. She was forced to lie but his ways and tactics made her think it was her idea, but she wasn't in control. He used his power advantage over her and shrouded her in fear, first mentally and then physically.

Zuby: That's just it. I hope this realisation will help you now.

Reena: It's scary. I was so vulnerable for so long.

Zuby: You were and to some extent you still are.

Reena: I really had no control whatsoever for such a long time.

Zuby: Exactly. I'm relieved that you finally understand that.

Reena: Woah, it's really sinking in now. I had no chance.

Zuby: I'm sorry, you really didn't. All those around you, all those with the power, put themselves first and left you to deal with things. You looked for affection; he saw that and took advantage. Then you survived for years, simply survived. But now you are beginning to thrive.

Reena: I think I'm beginning to see what you have seen from the moment I told you. I don't like what I can see; it's awful.

Zuby: What do you see?

Reena: A really vulnerable, fragile GIRL. An absolute monster that preyed on her. A family who weren't there. A situation that she had no hope of improving.

Zuby: That's why I had to help.

Reena: I really couldn't see it, I knew how I felt and I thought that you felt sorry for me, but looking in on what was is truly awful.

Zuby: But you have the courage to beat this. You don't realise how amazing you have been now and then. Reporting this, following it through.

Reena: I do need some time for this to settle a little. This new perspective is someone unnerving, frightening almost. Really genuinely understanding the situation I was in, the vulnerability, abandonment and the hurt, isn't nice.

Zuby: The fault is his, the shame is his and the blame is his. You are winning – you have much of what you deserve – safety, job, home and friends. You will continue to get all of the wonderful things you deserve because of your determination, strength and drive. I know it totally. I hope you believe it, too.

Reena: I'm trying, Zuby, I really am. When I tackle the deservingness I am met with a battle of 'Why do you deserve to feel that you deserve?'

Zuby: Because you were a little girl.

Reena: I apologised to her 1000 times for what happened.

Zuby: Are you able to say the same to your present self?

Reena: No 🙁

Zuby: But that little girl is you.

Reena: Yes, that makes sense. I don't know why I find it so hard.

Zuby: Because that's what was literally beaten into you.

Reena: 😭

Zuby: I hope you really can forgive yourself now.

Reena: These past few days, I've really genuinely come to terms with how young and defenceless I was. How I was so vulnerable and it was all so wrong, but I can't forgive myself.

Zuby: By not forgiving, you're blaming?

Reena: You're going to get really cross and disheartened now. Blame myself seems too strong but it's in that area. I don't know 😔 My head is a mess.

Zuby: What you said earlier, it goes back to the very beginning when we first started talking. You can't forgive yourself because you need control in your life. If you forgive yourself you have to admit that you weren't in control. You're not ready to admit that to yourself because it's frightening. In life no one is in control of everything. It's a fact. You have knowledge and experiences that you didn't have before so you can keep yourself safe. You will never allow this to happen again.

Zuby: You have to accept that at that time you weren't. You have to be brave enough to take that leap and trust that in future and in the present you can be in control of your safety in a way you couldn't have been back then.

Reena: I look back and realise how young and defenceless I was and how cruel it all was. But if I continue to think that way now, it begins to consume me; I have no control over it and I struggle to function. By taking charge of it, putting it onto me, allows me to take control of being able to leave it. It's odd; forgiving myself feels like I'm giving up, like I'm dropping down in my fight. Thinking I was somewhat deserving gives me some ownership, some control, some management of it. I'm disappointed with myself. I know you'll say I've made progress in other areas and I can see this logically but can't accept it or believe it. I hate that I was that girl. I really, really hate it. What if that is who I really am? Vulnerable and weak? Easy to manipulate and coerce? Stupid and naïve? And the more I try to fix myself, the more of that is revealed.

Zuby: So that is it. You feel you could still be vulnerable and weak. That someone might hurt you again. I understand.

Reena: It hasn't always been as damaging as of late but there has never been a day when I haven't thought about it.

Zuby: You've not really dealt with it before, you've coped. The period with your dad triggered this episode. If you deal with it you will never have to fear an episode again.

Reena: That's why I'm still fighting it; there really are times when it would be easier to not fight. I feel like I'm so close to unravelling. I just want to slump in a corner, wrap myself up and hide away.

Zuby: You've made some major, uncomfortable realisations in the last few days. So it's the impact of that. What will it look like? That's the part that scares me.

Reena: Slumped, not leaving the flat, being extremely upset and not being able to say why, and not being able to think straight.

Zuby: Now you have to take it one step forward: at 26 you are wiser, knowledgeable, determined and in control. You are not a victim; you are a survivor.

Reena: I'm not though, am I. I genuinely need the help that you're so kindly giving, the support from friends. It's not just nice it's literally needed.

Zuby: It IS needed and is the case for anyone that's been through what you have – that's normal.

Reena: I can see the progress in some areas. Why can't I move on from this? The simplest and most basic level, the one we've been working on the longest.

Zuby: Acknowledge the progress you have made.

Reena: What I meant was: I'm not fixing myself; I'm having to be fixed.

Zuby: Sue needed help when she was physically unwell – her broken arm? You need help because you are mentally unwell. You've been courageous from the beginning. As soon as you had some understanding you removed yourself, you were brave enough to report it, to go on with your life, to study and to chase your dreams. You're courageous now in fighting this. You've always been amazing. Do you see?

Reena: You know the answer.

Zuby: Don't you believe me when I tell you?

Reena: I believe that you think it.

Zuby: There are stories of people who don't report substance abuse and so on. You ARE NOT one of those. You're strong, determined and that's why you're healing.

Reena: It's exhausting.

Zuby: It's time to accept what was, to grieve and then
to embrace your future.

> Reena: Why isn't it working quicker? 😢 Sorry, that's
> not fair. I didn't mean that. Thank you for everything;
> for all of your precious time with me and the hours
> upon hours of research, your dedication throughout,
> your kind smile, always, and the constant effort you
> put in. Thank you so much. I wasn't in control,
> I wasn't to blame and it wasn't my fault. I didn't
> deserve any of it then. I deserve good things now.

The next counselling appointment with a more appropriately
qualified professional was imminent. Reena was terrified of going
because people at work had told her she would fall apart and be unfit
to work. It led to another low.

> Reena: Disgust, vulnerability and timidity, I think.

Zuby: Whom does the disgust belong to?

> Reena: At this moment in time, me.

Zuby: Look at your photos of that child.

> Reena: I feel young and vulnerable right now.

Zuby: Look at her in the eyes. Can you tell her (any
age) that she is disgusting?

> Reena: When the book asks 'How old did you feel?'
> in the chapter and 'How old do you feel now?', right
> now I feel that age and want to hide away.

Zuby: At that age, could you use the word 'disgust' and aim it at her?

Reena: No.

Zuby: We've spoken a lot about the past. The detail you have shared so bravely is horrific. I know you'll know more that you haven't shared but I can fill in the gaps. It was him, all him. The disgust, the crime and the abuse – it was him that was weak and manipulative. He was deliberate and responsible for his actions.

Reena: Thank you.

Zuby: You are a survivor. One of the estimated 25% of people who are abused. You are not alone but you are one of the few who is able to speak out, to share and to heal.

Reena: Hit me hard, yes... Think of a fly hit by a tanker that was hit by a freight train that was shunted by a jumbo jet. As good as you are at everything. There's nothing you can do right now. I do not want this appointment tomorrow. I don't want to go through thread to needle yet again. I don't want to be judged and to need help. I don't want to fall apart and completely uncoil what I've spent the last 13 years holding together. I don't want information taken back to work for sarcastic and nasty comments to be made. I don't want to tell it all again; I hate every part of this. I don't want my rollercoaster useless brain to spill everything.

I'll probably be fine in the appointment because I naturally hold it together in front of a stranger. Then I'll get in my car and I'll crumble, I'll fall apart and ask a million and one questions and hate myself even more. I don't want to be me anymore. I don't want my past, my problems or my issues. I don't want to deal with it.

We met up before the appointment – me in my car and Reena in hers. She shared the nightmare she had written down as part of her therapy.

"I couldn't tell you the information before because I knew you'd be repulsed by it. It might be time to go out with a bang. Not sure I'm fit for anything anymore," she said.

"Stop thinking like that. I was repulsed by him, not you. You're upsetting me."

"You shouldn't be because I'm not."

"I can't do this," I say.

"Then leave me, please. I don't want to show my face anywhere anymore. I want to hide away here where no one can see me and I can pretend I don't exist."

"Don't do this."

"You're not letting me down. It'll be in a better place without me, it's doing everybody a favour."

"We've spent so much time on the positives. Don't throw it away," I urged.

"I genuinely want to stop taking up your time."

"Then listen to me."

"I don't want to make you fight to help. I hope that you'll not put up the fight and just not help. I am sorry. I am such an awkward cow. All you do is try to help and I put up barrier after barrier. I am sorry. I'm awful and grotesque. I'm really struggling."

"I'm not going anywhere," I say. "I'm here. I'm staying to see you're alright. I'll be here when you come out."

It was late when the appointment ended. As she emerged from the ordeal, I got out of my car to greet her. She walked speedily to her car and drove away – not a word or glance between us. I was afraid of what might happen next so I literally jumped back into my car and followed her to her flat. We talked and she cried so deeply. I wished I could make it better for her but all I could do was hold her and tell her I was there for her. She did calm down and we talked about her progress. She began to see it and acknowledge it.

Day Thirty-eight

> Reena: Thank you for sitting by me and holding me before you left. You understand me more than anyone else; you understand the fight and the healing more than I do on most occasions. I know that you are not expecting miracles or overnight results.

Zuby: I have spent so much time trying to make
certain that anything I suggest is evidence-based, is
safe and will work where a person engages.

> Reena: It's just that it's tiring so I don't always want to do it. The 'not trying on' days also link back to not deserving, not deserving to heal.

Zuby: If you can't fight for you right now, then
fight for me. Fight because it matters. You have to
genuinely remove your internal barrier to healing.
You have to see you are a good person who went
through horrific times through no fault of your own.
Begin to rewrite your life today.

Reena: 👍

Zuby: Don't delete any more messages. One day you'll look back at your journey and we'll talk about what we did together.

Reena: Thank you for persevering with me, for not giving up on me. I'll not lie: this healing is hard; it's messy, all over the place and long. I yearn for one of my parents to be there and just hug me tight while I cry and be reassured by them. And that's when I realise what I don't have. I can have all the friends in the world, amazing ones who really listen, actively help and go out of their way to support me, all the while getting nothing back in return. And I feel as if I'm being unappreciative when I say I want a parent and I really don't mean to be at all. I can't say that I want my mum because she's always been rubbish. It was Dad that used to reassure and hug me through rough times, but I've lost that now. For crying out loud, I'm 26 years old, I should be able to deal with stuff on my own. But I can't and I'm having a negative impact on others now and it's out of order. I'm not giving in; I'm not. I'm just having one of those cries where I just need to get it out.

Zuby: Family is important always, but especially at difficult times. Like you said, they've never been there. In fact, they've always let you down.

Reena: They don't know it all.

Zuby: They never sat down and talked to you about what happened though, did they?

Reena: No.

Zuby: Did you tell anyone?

Reena: Bits.

Zuby: I don't understand that. After you moved in and this started, you never asked for help?

Reena: By the time I was back in touch with them it was just the norm.

Zuby: When you were 15, before you moved in, when they found out. They didn't do anything apart from tell you to choose them or him?

Reena: Correct. Mum'll be aware of a lot. She stayed friends with his ex-wife.

Zuby: I asked Jan if she knew he was violent; she said that would be believable, so she knew.

Reena: I'll never convince them that it wasn't my fault. I've given up on it.

Zuby: He was a grown man, bigger and stronger than you. He used his power to take away your control. He raped you. That's unforgivable.

Reena: Please don't use that word.

Zuby: I won't judge you negatively. You didn't have control, you couldn't say no.

Reena: That's one of the hardest parts to deal with, that's why it's taken so long to come out. Sorry.

Zuby: Bruises heal but the others leave mental scars, a feeling of total suffocating powerlessness. To be able to heal, you have to be able to speak about how you feel about all aspects, without fear of judgement.

Reena: Thank you.

Zuby: You need to be totally honest about how you feel. I'm here to listen and help. You were 13, just 13 the first time. A child. That's what you need to acknowledge.

Reena: I'm just hurt and I'm cross.

Zuby: You are safe, in control. You are healing. You are a survivor.

Reena: That doesn't change the fact that I feel hurt though, unfortunately. By him, by what he did, how he made me feel then and how he and it makes me feel now. And then I'm hurt now, hurt at the state I'm in and how I need help. I've got some amazing people around but I can't help but feel alone most of the time 🙁 What I really wish right now is that I had a mum. Not mine because she's never done that job.

Zuby: I know and I'm sorry but you can only control what YOU do, not others.

Reena: Realisation that I was really, really hurt, that I was so young, that I had no chance, that I was trapped and tricked and genuinely and stupidly believed the things he told me 😢. That it was me.

Zuby: All of that is true except that you weren't stupid. He tricked an inexperienced, trusting child. That is grooming and the violence is taking total control of you. This realisation is so important. It will eventually lead you to forgive yourself and to understand that you were not in control, not to blame.

Reena: One day we'll have time when we just chat and there's no fixing to be done.

Zuby: Yes, you deserve to be free of the past. I don't understand how he could inflict that on you. When I hear or see something that reminds me of what you went through, there is a deep gut-wrenching feeling I get. I have it now and it's there every time, without fail. He took away your childhood in the cruellest ways possible. The pain, suffering and fear you must have gone through makes me cry even to think about it. 'Haunting' is the right word.

Reena: Thank you for understanding.

Zuby: Just look at that photo – forgive her. Whatever happened, however you think it happened. Look at her – she's a child. She might have been intelligent and witty, but she's just a child. She doesn't know what love is, how it is supposed to be expressed. She doesn't know how cruel people can be. She's just a child.

Reena: Yes.

Zuby: That she is amazing to have survived, to have escaped, to make herself safe and in control?

Reena: Yes.

Zuby: Will you forgive her?

Reena: I still don't want to be me and what I am because of what happened.

Zuby: Can you forgive that little girl for doing what any child would have done in those circumstances? You are not what happened to you. You are amazing, good, compassionate, kind, funny and caring.

Reena: 'You are not what happened to you' – that's exactly it. I am. Tarnished because my innocence was lost so young. Damaged because I wouldn't say no. Shameful because it happened.

Zuby: You're so wrong, Reena. He stole your innocence; it wasn't 'lost'. It was done to you.

Reena: I hate that more.

Zuby: The little girl didn't say no because he, but he, lied to her. She didn't have the life experience to know that. Children are wired to trust. Her significant adults failed to educate her. The shame is his. He did it knowing it was wrong. Later, when you did say no, he punished you so you had to learn how to survive.

> Reena: No, but I know what was happening and what went on to happen.

Zuby: Be angry with him, be disgusted with him. Don't hurt her anymore. She escaped and deserves to be free.

Day Thirty-nine

Reena had had yet another nightmare, a new memory of a terrible event in her life. The re-experiencing was utterly draining.

Zuby: Whatever happened in your dream – you were brave enough to escape from him in reality. You're safe.

> Reena: I'm exhausted.

Zuby: I know. Hold on.

> Reena: From a selfish point of view, it would be easier to not be here.

Zuby: You are making progress and for you not to fulfil your potential would be a tragic waste. For you – forget about others.

Reena: It's how I feel on the inside, in my head, because of how I am and what I feel and think about myself. Let me try to explain: it's about what has happened, what I know about what has happened, how I can't get it out of my head and how the feelings are still so vivid. The amount of healing that has to be done, the fact that any healing has to be done; I'm cross about that part.

Zuby: I understand the anger. The feelings are real and justified but you're not going to be in that position ever again. I understand having that in your head everyday is so hard. There's a better way now. You're engaging in the process of healing. It's a long journey but at the end you will be able to be you again. You'll be able to make choices, be happy.

Reena: I'm saying that I know my past and I hate it that much. I won't lie; it's getting harder. I don't think I've ever sobbed the way I sobbed on you last night and I've done that a couple of times now.

Zuby: You should hate your past. It was horrific. But it doesn't define you. You decide that.

Reena: Concentrate on your family.

Zuby: Concentrate on my family while someone I know and care about might be alone contemplating suicide?!

Reena: You asked me directly, that's the only reason I said. Not contemplating.

Zuby: You have to believe me when I say he was an evil, sadistic bastard. That you are a survivor and stronger than that weak shit.

> Reena: Thank you. I'm so lucky to have found you. Your care and determination to help is like no other. I cannot thank you enough for the ways you are here for me without fail.

Day Forty

Zuby: I want you to know – that I hear what happened to you, that I believe you, that your feelings are valid. That I don't blame you for any of it, that I am not embarrassed or ashamed by anything you did to survive. I don't judge you. I judge him because he was in control.

> Reena: I need it all to be over, Zuby. It's not fair, I didn't ask for this.

Zuby: It's not your fault.

> Reena: It's all the crap that I'm too pathetic to deal with that upsets me. I'm just at the stage where I hate it all and it dawns on me that bit more that it really WAS me who went through all the stuff I write down, and I hate all of that, too. I just want happy memories and, yes, I know that's all coming, but I'm so fed up of my mind being full of awful things. No, I'm not there now and I'll never be there again but I want it out of my head, too, but it's as if that's too much to ask and I'm pathetic for not just being able to move on, but it genuinely haunts

me and it's changed me and I don't want it. He won't be curled up crying on a settee in a flat – he carries on and ignores what he did. Yet at 26, I'm left having to somehow rebuild my life and how my head works just to be able to get through the next 20 minutes. I'm 26 and I can hardly leave my flat to socialise. I'm surviving through pills, psychotherapy and advice following thoroughly read articles and research. I want to be well. I don't want to be a burden. I just want to be a normal friend who you choose to catch up with, who gives you energy instead of zapping it and who you are happy to leave and go home without worrying.

Zuby: The way you see yourself is all wrong. You amaze me with your resilience and remarkable strength, too.

Reena: I should be able to cope better. I'm pathetic.

Zuby: You're not pathetic. You're justifiably hurt by the trauma you endured. You're coping better than many. I'm telling you it's a fact – statistics back it.

Day Forty-one

Zuby: How are you feeling? Give me your pst.

Reena: I love myself. I deserve love. I forgive myself. People like me for who I am. I will not use negative terms towards myself. I will create a safe and bright future.

Zuby: Allow yourself self-compassion. Be honest; acknowledge how you feel but fight back whenever needed.

Reena: I will give it my all, I promise.

That night became our norm. Yet another memory re-emerged from the deep inside her mind. When it returned, it held nothing back.

Reena: Last night was like torture and I know full well that I am not there anymore and it was only a dream and that I wasn't physically hurt, but each of the nights take their toll. Being normal today was hard.

Zuby: I know it's impossibly hard. I really, really do. I don't expect everything to be **OK** overnight.

Reena: And I guess sometimes I don't want to talk about it or try and fix that part of it in my head. Some parts of this are just cr*p and that's it. If we're being honest, I'm thoroughly fed up of this now. No more. I'll finish the week and then I'll stay away from work. Then I'm out of sight for good.

Zuby: Hold on for all of those reasons we went through.

Reena: I do need you to know that I hugely appreciate everything.

Zuby: Tell yourself: my mind is processing the memories but I'm safe now. Whatever he did does not define you today. You deserve compassion; he deserves shame. Push it back to him. You survived and to survive you were and are unbelievably strong. I am so, so proud of you.

Reena: Your words mean a lot x

Zuby: Self-compassion encourages us to begin to treat ourselves and talk to ourselves with the same kindness, care and compassion we would show a good friend or a child.

Reena: I can't help the fear that when you know more you'll change what you think of me. And I would understand.

Zuby: What more is there?

Reena: Just the details I hold back. Like that dream.

Zuby: He was evil, pathetic and weak. There is nothing you have shared that makes me think any less of you.

Reena: Thank you.

Zuby: There is not even a tiny strand of what you've told me that makes me think negatively of you.

Reena: I find it hard to believe.

Zuby: He used his strength and he used force against someone physically unable to defend themself.

Reena: Did you read all the one I wrote last?

Zuby: I know now that that part is the worst part. It's in all of your dreams. It's what causes the greatest feelings of shame because it totally violates. We didn't talk about it at the start because it's so intimate. But now we do, and we can, because I understand.

Reena: I don't want anyone to know, that's just it.

Zuby: I'm sorry. Being heard is essential for healing. I want to hear whatever you want to say.

Reena: I believe you, I trust you. I truly, really, genuinely hate myself for what happened. I hate that I was beaten and scared and trapped and hurt over and over again. I hate that. But what really kills me inside and every single part of me is the abuse, the times that all control was taken from me and in ways I never imagined. I hate myself because he's touched me, I've felt his breath and heard his words. I really can't even say some of the words so I have to talk around it. There are some things that I cannot shift and that is one of them; knowing what he's done to me makes me despise myself.

Zuby: Despise HIM – he owns those actions. Hate him – he did those things. The words you can't say

– he did those things. He took away control but now
you are taking it back. Step by step, day by day. You
can. We will rid you of his shame.

> Reena: I always used to be quiet, kind and gentle.
> Now that I'm scared of people seeing the damage I
> adopt a loud, brash persona.

Zuby: True – sometimes you are a little brash but
the fact you are aware of that mode, and you know
it's a protective guise for you, means you can control
it. Acknowledge the emotions to heal. Understand
yourself so you can be kind to yourself: that's what
they mean when they say 'forgive yourself'.

> Reena: Thank you.

Zuby: The truth is that you are a survivor, a good
person who is strong, determined, kind, funny and
capable.

> Reena: I lived the physicality of it, yet the memories
> and feelings alone make me want to give in.

Zuby: I won't let you give in. You're healing. What
you did yesterday was honestly one of the bravest
things I've ever seen.

Day Forty-two

1.45 am and it was already a bad night.

> Reena: A really bad night. Nasty dreams. I walked and hit my nose and mouth on something.

Zuby: Your mind is processing the memories so that you can stop feeling the awful emotions attached to them. I know it doesn't feel like it, but this is part of the healing.

> Reena: I can't ground – help? X They're getting stronger and scarier.

Zuby: Make sure your feet are on the rug, flat, and sit back as much as possible at this stage.

> Reena: Yes.

Zuby: Then breathe really deeply, eyes open, so you're looking at something in your room. Count to min of 5. In your head, think about the numbers as you count… calmer?

> Reena: Yes.

Zuby: Keep breathing like that. Then as soon as you feel slightly calmer, begin the body scan. Focus on each muscle group. Picture the muscle groups in your head so that they are the image in your head. Be aware of your facial expressions – relax any frowning or tight jawline, etc.

> Reena: I'm OK now. Thank you.

Zuby: 'Shame is the lie someone told you about yourself.'[3]

Day Forty-three

A further twist was the occurrence of waking nightmares. The therapist called them 'flashbacks'. At any time, Reena could re-experience a past event whilst awake. I thought that this was it – she would have to leave work and might be sectioned.

> Reena: It's been a tough day, probably helped by lack of sleep and an awful dream. I had an awake flashback this morning – heard his voice at work and had to stop and ground and then again in the meeting. I feel like I'm going mad.

Zuby: You did brilliantly today. You're not going mad. This is you getting rid of the past by processing. https://www.beautyafterbruises.org/blog/flashbacks

> Reena: Like you keep reminding me. It's 2019, yet I can't simply relax as it comes to bedtime because he still haunts me. What he did still hurts me every night and then I spend the days fighting the hurt.

Zuby: That's something to be angry about, isn't it?

> Reena: I haven't set eyes on him for over a year and I haven't been under his control for 7 years. Yet I can recall what his grip feels like, how heavy he is,

how greasy his skin is, his stubble, his breath, his tone, his voice, the words he used, his expectations and thought patterns 🛐. It makes me sick every single night. I can't escape.

Zuby: Tell me about that anger. I'm listening.

Reena: I don't have any memories growing up after 14 other than him. I can remember all the hurt, the abuse, I can feel him and hear his words. I don't know what it's like to grow up and build social circles but I know exactly what it's like to be terrified to say no. To cower as I walk past him. To have all control taken and be completely powerless as he decides what he wants and to take.

Zuby: You are right to be angry that he stole those years and experiences from you – for years and years he deprived you of what any other child could expect. Say it. I'm listening.

Reena: I hate him. He ruined my life. I may have achieved x, y and z but I've had to work so much harder. He's got away scot-free; despite being his toy at his disposal for several years, I'm the one sat suffering. Because of him, my friends think I'm a misery guts enjoying feeling sorry for myself. I'm angry because he made me feel powerless – then and now. I'm angry because he rejected all my efforts to appease him and because my family rejected me. I'm angry because I had needs and expectations of him that he shattered time and time again in the cruellest of ways. I'm angry because he violated my mind and my body. I'm angry because I had to become a different person to survive and I still haven't found myself.

Zuby: He was evil, pathetic and weak. He could never have been with you had he not controlled you. He made himself feel big by sharing his cruelty with other abusers. He couldn't get validation anywhere else. He lied to you, groomed you and emotionally abused you by constantly belittling you. He sexually abused you and raped you repeatedly. He imprisoned you through his lies. Then he used you for his self-gratification as if you were his property, a piece of meat. He hurt you till you bled, till you cried and till you screamed out. That makes ME angry.

Reena: Thank you.

Zuby: But despite his actions – his sadistic, criminal, immoral acts – you escaped. You took control. You achieved and are still achieving. You have made a life worth living – you'll have a legacy. He can't have any of that. I'm sorry that this happened to you. Proud that you survived, that you lived and are living and that nothing can stop you.

Reena: I'm livid that he gets to live his life exactly how he shapes it yet I'm left living mine as he has sculpted it. I have to fight night and day to build and shape my own. It's not fair. I'm angry because he knew how much power he had, he knew I was timid and would listen to him anyway, but he still hurt me to make sure I would never say no. He didn't need to do that. He shouldn't have. I'm angry because I lost all of those years and I can never get them back. I spent time learning the wrong type of life lessons, how to keep an impossible person happy, how to duck and dive from being hurt and how to wriggle out of being held up, but no skills on how to socialise growing up and how to have healthy relationships. I'm angry because I was left fighting all alone. People who did know and could have helped didn't. And people who would have helped had already abandoned me and were no longer interested. I'm angry because at 26, despite having built my own life, reaching my goals and having hope for the future, I have to put my life on pause yet again to clear up the mess he created. He took away my teenage years so I could be his toy and now he's taking away my adult years while he's left living his life how he chooses, each day. I'm pissed off because 13 years after he first laid his hands on me, I'm left blaming myself for all of it. His actions and words made me believe that I was so inadequate that I still believe I have little to no worth and low self-esteem.

Zuby: But now you are learning that you have the strength to heal.

Reena: Thank you for all of your help and support along the way. There are many times where you could have stepped away and no one would have thought twice, but you've really stood by me and spent hour after hour trying to find what was needed. You've stood by my side and held me, often literally, and have rebuilt me from hitting rock bottom and squeezed all of my broken pieces back together with your hugs. I'm so glad I found you.

Zuby: Know this much – you are an amazing person. You will get through this because of your determination. Experiencing flashbacks does not mean that you are losing your mind. It means that you are at a point in your life where you are able to deal with things that perhaps you couldn't cope with earlier. Flashbacks tend to lose their intensity once you have assembled the fragments into a coherent memory, talked about it, cried about it and absorbed the memory into your life.

Reena: Thank you x again. A thousand thank yous will never be enough. So why on earth can't I deal with the rubbish in my head and fight it? I've fought for my life before. Why can't I do it when I have a life to fight for 😢😢. My life was this: running round making sure the house was clean, the bills were paid, the food was on the table, the cupboards were full and that the child was happy – MIGHT this have stopped it just once? Just once, saying the right thing to him might have pleased him. Not daring to answer though, just in case it's the complete wrong thing and then it spirals out of control again. Have you ever messed up something and felt really stupid for about 5 minutes or so? Burning up red, wanting-the-ground-to-swallow-you-up kind of stupid? Replace that with shame and disgust, but it doesn't just last 5 minutes, it lasts an eternity. I still wish that the overdoses had worked or that one day he'd gone too far because then it would have stopped and I wouldn't have this to fight. At the moment I feel that I'm barely surviving so it wouldn't be a waste.

Zuby: But you need to remember you were a child; you don't appear to have been given any guidance from your adults. Seems to be a case of 'go and find out'.

Reena: And I accept that I was stupid for staying. I know that was wrong now, I've learnt that.

Zuby: Not stupid. You didn't have the knowledge you have now. You know how people live and how relationships are supposed to work – back then, you didn't. The biggest thing is for you not to feel shame. I've told you so many times why but it won't stick. No matter what I say or the evidence I present.

Reena: I've moved to a point where I question whether I should feel shameful and disgusting.

Zuby: That's the reason I first hugged you. So you could see I didn't think anything that happened to you disgusted me.

Reena: It might help... Imagine wearing a white dress and someone holds you down and squirts ketchup all over you, you can't change and you know you didn't stain your dress but you feel stupid and embarrassed walking around with ketchup on you. Replace stupid and embarrassed with shame and disgust. It's really hard trying to explain it. That 'stain' happened to me so I am both those things.

Zuby: I understand that part. He violated you in the most intimate of ways. He did it again and again. Sometimes, to survive, you made it seem you accepted it from him. Other times you fought back or said no. It made no difference. I do get that.

Reena: It kind of moves on from that then on, and because the shameful and disgusting happened to me, I am those things. It happened to me. That remains a fact, regardless of the situation, circumstances, blame, fault or choosing to do so; he did it TO ME. And therefore that shame and disgust sits on me.

Zuby: No. It should read like this: HE DID IT to me so the shame and disgust sits with him.

Reena: It's the 'happening to me' part.

Zuby: It did not just happen. A CONTROLLING, EVIL PERSON CHOSE TO DO IT TO WHOMEVER HE COULD COERCE.

Reena: Yes.

Day Forty-four

People at work are jealous.

Zuby: You heard what they said at work? I don't want anything from you. Just in case she put doubt into your mind.

Reena: Never.

Zuby: It is therefore one of the most difficult feelings to shift because it is that person (so they think). It's a characteristic they've given themselves, feeling it is like the colour of their skin, i.e. almost genetic. Is that correct?

Reena: My ketchup explanation didn't cut it then? 😳

Zuby: It is wired into your brain. So you think it's a fact. Like you know you have ginger hair, pale skin, are female, etc. But the difference is that it is not an inherited characteristic of yours. We have to rewire your brain. Start by telling yourself the positives. Say: I am loveable because I am kind and considerate. I am proud of achieving x, y and z.

Reena: It's not that I fight the solution. There's so much work involved in getting to the solution that I realise how inadequate I am and I'm disappointed with myself. It's absolutely nothing that you do. I'm truly sorry. I really am sorry. I appreciate all of your help and I promise I will use it all. I am sorry I struggle with it.

Zuby: That's what the book says. You're used to self-hate, you can't see another way. You're afraid of how it would feel not to be like that. You will have to express, in depth, your: sadness, anger and every specific feeling you have associated with shame. When you can do that, you will have truly acknowledged your emotions and you will understand self-compassion in the true sense.

> Reena: I am getting better, I am committed to all of the strategies and really do desperately want to be better; I will get there. Is it OK for things to be too much sometimes? Is it OK to just want some time and space to say things were awful and, in that moment, not try and fix it all and find the positives? Can we just take time to acknowledge that, once, things were dreadful and incredibly unfair?

Zuby: Yes, it really is, but remember the positives – that you did nothing wrong, that you can be proud of yourself. The shame and disgust is his. He did those things either through lies, threats or his strength. The most powerful way to tackle this – rid yourself from his shame.

> Reena: I'm determined to get better. I won't give up, I promise. Shall I be honest?

Zuby: Always.

> Reena: OK, if you really want the truth, this is rubbish. Not only is it rubbish, it's downright unfair. I don't want to cry the woe is me tale, but

I've suffered enough, he made damn well sure of that. But apparently, my brain doesn't think that's enough; 10 years and more later it gives me crippling nightmares, daytime flashbacks, agonising anxiety and rubbish moods. It's not fair and I want rid.

Zuby: Then be rid – use the strategies – why don't you? Are you afraid of letting go of the rubbish? Does that feel safer than the unknown?!

Reena: Be cross with me. I can take it. Shout, use capitals, send several messages and put me in my place. Get cross, tell me off and get it off your chest.

Zuby: Where is your commitment to yourself? It's often tough. It's tough for me, too – yes, it's an entirely different kind of tough but it is tough. But I go on and on and on. I don't walk away. Well maybe I want to stop when it gets tough, too.

Reena: My commitment is day in, day out. When I get out of bed every day I try and convince myself I'm worth having a shower and try not to despise the body I'm in. It continues when I try and function despite having had a dreadful night of being reminded of the crap I lived with. Then there's a bit more commitment to feed myself when I convince myself I'm worth using food on. Then I fight to read those sheets that tell me what's good in my life and I smile for half a second. Then mostly I realise I've got the rest of the day on my own with the person I'd rather not be, oh, and then there might be a flashback or two which makes me think I'm weaker than ever and my mind is crumbling. I'll speak to a friend all the while wondering if I'll be able to keep a lid on it or whether I'll boil over and hurt her. But still I carry on through the day and it's another one to tick off being closer to the end. Then when I've fought all day and I'm exhausted and wonder if it really would just be easier and better for everyone to just give in, it's coming to bedtime to be free of all these thoughts that would be bliss, to recharge me for the next day. But instead, I go through it all again, sometimes remembering abuse I'd forgotten.

Zuby: You know where you are, you also know the truth; you know how to get from one to the other. But you fight trying to get there. You know, factually, a child can't be blamed for what happened but you still hate yourself for it. You should be fighting that with everything within you. I feel like I have to fight you to help you. Like you're not on my side, sometimes. Like you believe him more than you believe me. Like I can never show you enough kindness or compassion although I go overboard on a daily basis. It's never enough. It's like I'm fighting him through you and you listen to him but not to me. You understand his language; you don't understand mine. Care, compassion, love, facts and evidence – that's all I know. But it's not enough, is it?

Reena: I don't put him first.

Zuby: You use his words to fight mine. I've never asked you to believe anything I've said. Instead, I meticulously give you evidence, research and help. But you counter all of that with his words. You believe him. He's done a better job of convincing you than I seem to be capable of.

Reena: No.

Zuby: If you listen to his words over mine then it's game over.

Reena: Is this where we stop and part ways?

Zuby: It is your choice. I promised you that I'd never abandon you. I don't break my promises.

Reena: I won't cause you the hurt I have, I don't deserve your compassion or care – you're right, no one has ever given me that like you have. So leave me to rot in the thoughts I don't fight hard enough for.

Zuby: Don't use his words to battle mine. Don't let his methods win over mine. Make your choice. I'll respect it. Do the right thing for you, not the right thing for him. Tell me in the morning.

Day Forty-five

Reena: Then I want your way.

Zuby: And I'm here. Stop using his lies and his language of hate, violence, belittling and control to argue against my words of kindness, compassion and truth. I don't think I can defeat both of you. I can beat him, but not both of you together.

Reena: I am on your side. Always.

Zuby: Then stop using his words. Stop giving his voice credence. So, the language you used yesterday – was that what he put there or what you WANT to think about yourself?

Reena: It's not what I want to think about myself.

Zuby: So admit it, the consequences of your emotional flashback yesterday were to reinforce his words?

Reena: Yes. How do I stop myself getting into those states where it's as though I don't have control?

Zuby: Let's think logically. For the first time – you know what an emotional flashback is. It's where your emotions revert to the emotions the 13- to 18-year-old felt but couldn't express. Now you know how to express them rationally and without fear of punishment. So breathe, remind yourself of the year, your age and your freedoms. Only then, after grounding, express your feelings.

Reena: So I can stop and ground in the middle of a conversation?

Zuby: Whenever you choose. There are to be no more punishments, derogatory remarks, no hurting, hitting or abusing you. You can speak without fear. This goes right back to something I said a while back. Flashbacks are either the mind processing or attempting but failing to process. Where it fails, you can help it by talking it through. Won't be easy but it will resolve it.

Reena: Remember that YOU are the only person who has ever helped me to fight this. Thank you for being someone who hasn't judged me. Remember all the time you've taken to carefully push me but have never let me fall. YOU have shown me the compassion and love that people can have and YOU ALONE have made me pick my head up and look at the horizon, YOU have forced me to see what I can have in my own future. It is because of YOU that I will not give up this fight until it is won. But then, how can it be you that I hurt?

Zuby: You'll push and push and push till I can't do it anymore. Then you'll have fulfilled your own prophecy. I've read the research. It's what you're doing because that's what the research says. You push people away by hurting them.

Reena: I need to get better at grounding my emotions before interacting.

Zuby: You're right, that an emotional flashback means you're at least 10 years younger mentally and you respond as such.

Reena: Does your book have a fast forward chapter?

Zuby: You need to improve on using everything we've shared. You know it is literally everything that's available. Nothing new has come from drs or counselling.

Reena: It's not an exaggeration to say that you have saved my life.

Zuby: We need to take this to a successful conclusion, don't we? Together, I think we will ☺

Reena: Can we make an agreement that whatever is discussed we will not part on sour terms? I know I'm often hard work and you want to pull your hair out; if you need to be cross please do be but, if possible, please don't leave being cross or without having brought it up and we have tried to fix it.

Zuby: We've been through too much to fall out. You were courageous and you did everything that was needed. Goodnight. Know that you own no shame or disgust. That instead you are a beautiful human being inside and out. 'It may feel like there are a million reasons to stand still and keep silent, but there are millions more to speak the unspeakable and move forward.'[4]

Reena: Thank you. It just feels like it's been a while since these emotions and memories have been this raw and I've forgotten what to do with them. I'm at the stage before crying; it's hard to explain. I hug you tightly for several reasons: because you make me feel safe, because you're doing so much for me and I know it hurts you and you need to be hugged too, because I need to say thank you and because I'm relieved that you don't run away and despise me after our conversations. I didn't realise I held on so noticeably tight, I'm sorry.

Zuby: I'm never going to run away because of what you tell me.

Reena: I do trust you, you do make me feel safe, but in these last few days you have astounded me that you haven't walked away.

Zuby: Why would I?

Reena: Because you know right from wrong, you know what acts are despicable, you have morals and you live a good life making right choices.

Zuby: You weren't in control of those acts. You were abused, exploited, tortured and raped. You were innocent.

Reena: Sorry, it's late; you don't want to discuss these things at this time. I'm just saying that I appreciate you and your care beyond words. What he did, it made me bad.

Zuby: No! You weren't able to control it; you were a victim, Reena. Let me use the right words. He raped you repeatedly. He hurt you more when you resisted, he hurt you when you didn't resist. You had no control. A victim can't be made bad by the actions of a perpetrator. The acts were bad, he used you and violated you in the most brutal ways. He used your body for his pleasure and sexual satisfaction. He used you; he forced you. He used that stun gun, knives and the rest. You are NOT bad.

Reena: I'm safe now.

Zuby: Yes. He did that to you. You had to survive so sometimes you stayed silent and I think that's why you blame yourself.

Reena: But sometimes I was nice to him. It's my shame.

Zuby: The shame is his because he committed crimes against you. Please don't blame her. She was just 13 when he began. Please don't put the shame or disgust on her; she is my friend. Tell her she can let go of the shame and disgust. Please. Does anything I say make a difference?

Reena: It is helping a lot – the way you make me say the words I hate, the way you're adamant I am not to blame and the way you will still be in my vicinity despite what you know.

Zuby: Society now understands and believes that when a person is overpowered into doing something against their will, without being asked, with the use of violence, force, strength or manipulation, then the person that happens to is INNOCENT, BLAMELESS AND WITHOUT FAULT. The PERPETRATOR has total ownership of the SHAME AND DISGUST.

> Reena: Zuby, please, please believe me when I say I want rid of this more than anything, I really do. I'll keep fighting, I promise. Some days it's so tough that I really do want to give up but I promise I won't.

Zuby: I think today has been one of the most difficult days because I can't get you to see that you own no shame. I've tried and tried and tried. I've willed it to happen but it won't. I don't want to see you in this state anymore.

> Reena: I have spent years attached to this shame, years believing it, living it and accepting it. There's a question where there wasn't before, there's doubt where there was none, there's drive to relinquish it which I never even knew was possible or worthwhile. All that within the short amount of time we have been talking – all BECAUSE OF YOU.

Zuby: You have the words; you're being heard. But you, yourself, can't accept that you were a child, a victim and helpless. You, yourself, can't accept that you did EVERYTHING possible even though you

have the mental scars to prove it. Until YOU accept
it, we just keep trying.

> Reena: I've got fight back, which I had lost.

Zuby: Tell the inner critic how you now recognise its
lies – whether it's in the form of a negative voice or
feeling. Nurture your inner child. She was right all
along. She was right to be hurt and scared but now
she is accepted, loved and safe. She is valued and
cherished.

> Reena: It takes a while to realise that when you say
> the present you're referring to now. It's as if now is
> the future and then is the present. But only for a bit,
> not for long.

Zuby: Healing is about accepting the past and
grieving for it because of its horror and then
focusing on the hope you have in the present and
future. 'A moment of self-compassion can change
your entire day. A string of such moments can
change the course of your life.'[5] Shame is his lie.
We're going to crush it.

> Reena: That realisation – he objectified me. I hate
> how that word makes me feel, as if I was just that
> for so long. As if that was the beginning and end
> of my worth and I didn't see through it – I let it
> happen. She's right, I feel sick when I think how the
> older I became the less 'nice' he was. I'm devastated
> that I was used and seen in one way for so long.
> What he was. Some things I can't say yet.

Zuby: Please say everything. I want you to say whatever you feel, without fear or worry. I'm willing you to have your words heard. I want to validate them. Remember, you didn't let it happen, HE made it happen. When you were a child, he groomed you, lied to you. When you were older, he controlled you totally. Everything I have done has only been possible because of the courage you've had to talk to me. Lack of control means all of the shame and blame belongs to the liar and the one who had the power. The shame is 100% his. He made this happen with a plan he put into place for years, deliberate and evil.

Nightmare: in that nightmare you were just 16 and 16 is so young. You can't think she could have fought off a grown, angry monster. She couldn't have run, pushed him away or screamed louder. He would have hurt her even more. So she did what she did to survive. She didn't leave, go to her parents or report it because she didn't know how. She was scared. She thought his lies were true, that he loved her, that if she could do better he might be kinder.

> Reena: Yes. I'm fighting. I think I'm on top of it all and have all the energy needed for the fight, ready to go again when needed… and then something happens 😟. And I just want to bury my head, cover my ears and hide away from everything.

Zuby: Here are the reasons for putting you through the writing: 1) as you write, you dissociate the negative emotions because you know it's not going to happen again; 2) to get it out of your head to allow processing, and 3) to see if any themes or issues arise. Love yourself at 26. You know more, you know better. You know your strengths and you know that no one is perfect and that's normal. You know the shame within you is a cruel lie, beaten into you. You know it's time to fight it and truly believe that it is not a part of you.

> Reena: OK, I'll think on it.

Later that day:

> Reena: I'm so lucky and words will never describe how grateful I am that you took a chance on me. I feel shiny and clean, like the dust has lifted away. I don't feel shame.

Zuby: Really?

> Reena: Yes, I'm smiling and I'm going to go shopping. Thank you for being everything I never had, all in one person.

She went shopping, went for a walk, had a pleasant afternoon and texted me now and again to tell me that she was doing well. Evening time:

> Reena: I can't share what I feel when I don't know myself. All I want to do is cry and it won't come. It's gone. The dirt has settled again.

Zuby: You've had that feeling once now, you're rewiring. I've told you many times. The development of your emotional centres has been stunted. But it can be and is being repaired. You need to do all of what you feel and I'll pick out your feelings and separate them from the things he told you to feel.

> Reena: I don't want a full flashback in front of you.

Zuby: Blaming yourself can be a way for you to feel more in control now. But it can't work in the long term because you don't deal completely with your loss. You just get stuck in shame and guilt. That total loss of control back then is so difficult to deal with now. But you have to believe that you do have control now.

> Reena: I promise I'll work as hard as I possibly can.

Zuby: We are born to be what we want to be within the constraints of our contexts. We must educate ourselves to remove any shackles. Then we can make choices, take responsibility and be accountable.

> Reena: Frustration at what you said is really clicking and ringing true but then that's going backwards. Dreams and flashes came back last night. Realising just how much Mum and Dad contributed to my lack of self-worth.

Zuby: The power of the mind is immense. I know the person you are and I accept everything about you. You should, too. Self-love suffocates toxic shame. You must accept who you are.

Reena: I won't give in.

Zuby: We're not far from the end. Everything I'm reading tells me once you have the awareness of what toxic shame is then you can get rid of it. Self-compassion is the answer. Just need you to apply that.

Reena: I understand.

Zuby: It makes me sad to think that what you actually think when you look in the mirror is what you wrote on the left-hand side of the page. But all of that is lies. His voice and his lies.

Reena: I'm sorry.

Zuby: I don't want you to be sorry. I want you to realise and throw it back to him. Ram it down his throat and choke him to death.

Reena: I know.

Zuby: How wonderful is that? To know the feeling that's hurt you the most, all of your life, was a lie and it can now go forever. Frustrated – wrote a letter to her:

Dear Serena,
You probably won't read this; I'm not worth your time:

I trusted him and thought he loved me. He said he would take care of me. I found out he lied to me.
He hurt me and I'm still afraid. I wanted to cry and shout but I wasn't allowed to then. I still hurt and I want someone to hear me. I'm so scared of what will happen next. I'm so afraid of everyone; if they knew what I am, they'd never come near me. I'm angry, too – I want my mum but she sees what I am and she keeps away, too.
Why me? Am I really such a bad person? I'm stuck here and I can't escape. There isn't anyone I feel safe with. I feel alone. There is no one to help me.
I try my best, I work so hard but it's not good enough for you, is it, Serena? Please help me; please be the one who holds me tight and keeps me safe. Please.

Love
Your Inner Child

> Reena: Thank you so much for this morning, I keep tearing up with happy tears.

Zuby: That's amazing. I'm so pleased.

> Reena: I feel fresh. I can feel again and I'm not hidden away under dirt and dust. I feel taller, brighter in appearance and lighter.

Zuby: Dear Serena,
Something amazing happened. Someone heard my cries for help – it was you. You allowed me to breathe for the first time. I have a longing to tell you

why I call out to you every day but you don't want
to hear, do you? I'm weak, that's what you think.
When you took the time to listen, I felt safe. I liked
how it felt.
I'm hurting and I need someone to help me. I want
it to be you. Only you can understand but even you
don't want me, do you?

Love
Your Inner Child.

I've always known that you're courageous but now I
realise that it takes real guts to let down your guard
and tell a stranger your deepest fears. You did that
and shone a light onto the shame. All I did was see
that the light clearly and without doubt identified
the shame as his.

Reena: Flashback .

Zuby: It's OK, just processing.

Reena: I'm OK.

Zuby: I have some good news – that dark cloud
called shame is a big lie – push it away forever.

Reena: It feels further away than ever. I feel really
fragile and vulnerable.

Zuby: You feel that because you listened to your
emotions from the past – they're painful. It will
return. You're rewiring. You've realised that shame

wasn't an inherent part of you. Over the last few days you've had that feeling a number of times. It's just a feeling – it's not part of you so you can choose to reject it. You listened to your inner child. You accepted her feelings, you nurtured and you were self-compassionate.

Day Forty-six

A nightmare…

> Reena: I can't promise I always have the words. Despite what you think, I do try every single day and every single session.

Zuby: You don't want pity, you've said it many times, but sometimes it's as if that's just what you've sunk into – the negativity – and lost all sight of the progress.

> Reena: I'm damn well ready to realise the positives and I'm desperate for this crap to be over. No one is more desperate than I am for a normal life, not even you. In the middle of this whirlwind of rubbish and intense healing the positives actually feel very few and far between in amongst all the tears, images and then the fallouts. I haven't lost sight of any progress. Every time I take one step in the right direction it feels like all I am faced with is the next uphill climb.

Zuby: Whilst you hold on to the false feeling of shame, you believe his lies and not me or the research.

Reena: Need to say something…

Zuby: Go ahead, please; you're worrying me.

Reena: There is a reason my sleep hasn't been as good the last couple of nights. I didn't want to lie to you about the change in sleep pattern. This coming week always hurts, it's the date that the grooming moved to more than talking and the memories always intensify, so this year seems that bit more difficult. My mind has been playing tricks on me and I only hope it calms down when I'm through with this week.

Zuby: You told me it was the November you were 14. Thank you for telling me. Were you 13? As I've seen your photo at 13. You're just a little girl. It's sick that he did that. I know that at 13 meant he started grooming you earlier. I don't know when. It means your parents didn't supervise you when you were even younger.

Reena: You're cross and upset ☹.

Zuby: I've said it so many times, you were just 14;
I've said it many times and you never corrected me.

Reena: I didn't have the heart to correct you as 13 sounds so much worse even though it's just a year.

Zuby: You were 12 in the photo on your dad's windowsill. You were tiny.

Reena: 😖

Zuby: It means they neglected you for longer; your nightmare began earlier.

> Reena: I've wanted to tell you a few times, then when it came to it I couldn't. I'm seeing him during the day 😟. What's happening to me? I'm scared.

Zuby: We'll talk and we'll resolve it. I have ideas. Remember, you are safe now. Remind yourself he is a coward, weak and insignificant. Now you have the power. You need to renew that determination. You're free, safe and you are educated about what happened. You know you're not to blame and that the shame is a lie. You know you always had real worth and that the way he treated you says everything about him and not about you. Fight.

Zuby: Dear Serena,
Finally, you're starting to listen. Is it really safe for me to talk or will that make you leave me like everyone else does? I know I'm not good enough. I know it was my fault. Those times when I let him, the times I didn't fight or even make a sound. I'm disgusting – that's what I deserved. But it hurt; he hurt me even though I tried my best. I'm just not good enough. I was so stupid, who would fall for his words except someone who was bad. I know it's who I am but I hate myself.
I'm pathetic – I want to cry because I think it hurt, but it's normal, isn't it? I'm weak. Everyone else gets on with life.

Sometimes, I'm terrified of what will happen next,
but that's because I'm weak too, isn't it?
I feel hurt. I feel shame. I feel anger. I feel sadness
and I feel breathless with fear. But that's all because
I'm weak. Anyone else would get on with life.
I know I'm a burden. I'm sorry.

Your Inner Child

But now you deserve to have your life back. Because
you are a survivor. You know the truth now. You
reject his lies; you accept their neglect was just
that. You are educated about how and why things
happened. We can do shame reduction work by
writing and talking about it. We can express them,
clarify them and connect with them. We spent time
talking about what happened and I hugged you for
what seemed like the longest hug.

Reena: I understand but the part I played.

Zuby: Let me start you off: he lied to you from the
beginning, so everything you believed about yourself
is wrong. Next?

Reena: It wasn't my fault; he had control so holds
the shame. I don't like knowing it.

Zuby: In processing, you must learn the lessons
so you can live with the memories without them
destroying you.

Reena: You're much stronger than I am x They stop me in my tracks whilst you always have a solution x

Zuby: You survived. I don't know anyone as strong as you.

Reena: You just are. You have every right to walk away but you want to help. You have a family, an important job and many commitments yet you read hour upon hour to help me. You come back time and time again and you understand when I struggle to engage. I don't always, in fact I rarely give the right answers, but you haven't given up on me and you do everything to help me get there.

Zuby: You should have had people who looked out for you at 13, 14, 15, 16, 17 and 18. Before, too, and now. You deserve someone.

Reena: Thank you for being someone. And thank you for educating me in what I deserve and what I should never accept.

Zuby: What we know about the following years proved that your feelings were always right but that he played with your mind and confused your emotions. Now you know you are vindicated. No one will ever hurt you like that again because now you have all the knowledge and understanding that you didn't have then.

Reena: Thank you.

Zuby: The hurt is justified. You need to listen to your inner child more than ever. Let her tell you how she feels. You need to respond to the needs in this memory. She's just realised that she was lied to from the beginning, that she went back thinking she was just being silly (because that's what he told her). That she went back because she believed him, thinking he would love her and look after her but in the years to come he did the exact opposite. That her so-called caregivers abandoned her to him. She wants to know why he would lie to her: he even said sorry. Now she knows even that was a lie. Tell her she was just an innocent little girl and that none of it was her fault. Show yourself compassion. It's not just fluffiness. Actually, it's: strength, courage, warmth, kindness and empathy. When you try to tackle the shame, you will draw on the feelings of compassion you have just made tangible and not attack yourself.

Reena: It's disgusting to read.

Zuby: These are your thoughts. Your feelings are not disgusting – can't be.

> Reena: He's completely stolen from me. All you said about being special and gentle – never. I was tiny; he's sick. I didn't have any of the features that men are said to be attracted to, yet he was and behaved as if so. How long had he actually been planning what he wanted? He knew what to say to trick me. I try talking about having a family but in reality the thought makes me ill. All I want to do is sob about

the whole thing. When I wake up from the dream I can really feel the pain. I don't understand how someone can want to do that to another person 😖.

Zuby: Your feelings are normal. He has stolen from you – I can't make that sound better. But I can say, when you find someone special, they will make you feel the way you should. I promise. Why does talk of a family make you feel ill?

Reena: Of having a husband.

Zuby: You mean of being intimate with him?

Reena: Pretty much.

Zuby: You know that's normal, don't you? When victims understand what happened, they find it difficult to trust. It's OK. I promise. You will learn to trust again. To love again in a normal way. You will understand that sex is a normal, healthy part of a relationship. You know how to keep yourself safe. You know what you deserve now. You would recognise anyone trying to trick you. You have never been safer because of all the knowledge and understanding you've developed.

Reena: How do I stop crying?

Zuby: Don't. Talk about how you feel. Talk and talk. Let someone hear and validate so you know you're right to cry.

Reena: I don't know how I can live with this.

Zuby: Because it's over. You survived and now, in 2019, you have never been safer, more in control or more aware of your worth.

Reena: I want to be sick.

Zuby: You can release yourself from the incorrect belief that the shame was ever yours. You've talked; it will get better now.

We spoke about the nightmares and I read them and she reacted to them. We stopped several times when she couldn't go on any further.

Zuby: You fought for the freedom you have today. No one helped you – you did it. You didn't do that to be like this now. You did it to be happy.

Reena: I just want to be free.

Zuby: You can be. That is the amazing truth. You can be because all the bad beliefs you hold onto are lies. The truth is that you are a joy. A wonderful person who shines and be proud to be seen by the world.

Reena: What do I do when all I want to do is cry?

Zuby: You cry and let someone hear why you feel that way. You have your tears and words validated. Then you can move into the present.

Reena: There's the bit that was in Sammy's book about how he got more violent more ways more often as I stopped looking so much like a child 😔. A bit more of a realisation of what he thought my worth was.

Zuby: It doesn't matter what he thought. He was an animal. An inadequate excuse of a human being.

Reena: That fits with what he thought my worth was.

Zuby: You invested everything in him. You have a huge sense of betrayal. That, too, hurts but you must realise it was never you. It was his immorality.

Reena: I hate him.

Zuby: He betrayed you; hurt you. He was so weak he needed to overpower a child. He is nothing in the present. You have to see him for what he really was rather than the person you invested your emotions in.

Reena: I agree. I agree with all of it. I'm more cross that some of that can't be remedied now.

Zuby: You should be cross. Furious at what he has done to you! The focus has to shift from him to you.

Reena: Yes.

Zuby: Today you are safer, in control, worthy and respected.

Reena: Yes, I am.

Zuby: Go to your compassionate mindset whenever possible. Love yourself because you are a good person inside and out. Summarise the learning from today, please.

> Reena: That he is revolting but that never reflected my worth. My caregivers were rubbish and neglectful but that was never a reflection of my worth. Is that alright?

Zuby: Yes. Perfect. You deserve apologies from all your caregivers for their many mistakes. Whether they are strong enough to offer them or not doesn't change anything regarding your worth. It's a reflection of how weak they are, even now. I'm sorry for that but remember: you're not alone. You are strong enough to create a happy fulfilling life without them.

> Reena: I wanted to vocalise but I couldn't. When I shouted stop I didn't mean you, I meant everything.

Zuby: You did so well with the dissociation. Then you fell apart. You collapsed on me. I had to hold you up. I don't think I've ever seen you that upset. And I couldn't understand it because you did so well with the dissociation. I thought I'd broken you.

> Reena: I managed the task better than the day before. Then we had finished, I think, and I just couldn't settle from them all, it was like they were consuming me.

Zuby: It's OK to cry. It's supposed to help but you need to talk. I know how difficult it is for you. I've read the testimonials of hundreds of people and most of all I've listened to you. But there's nothing about how the friend is supposed to react or deal with things.

Reena: You always do the right thing.

Zuby: We have the answers. Please hold on. It's just a matter of time now to the rewiring. You said the grounding is improving, I can see the dissociation is improving. When you do it really well, the dream doesn't even return that night.

Reena: You're right.

We talked and she shared her latest dream.

Reena: You practically ran home.

Zuby: You just described to me nothing short of a torture scene.

Reena: I'm sorry 😔.

Zuby: I can't imagine what must have been going through your head as it happened and I can't imagine what you did in the hours after. Did he show any regret? That's what usually happens — apologies and 'It'll never happen again'.

Reena: No. Cross during. Said this would sort things. Then after he carried on with normal stuff.

Zuby: I'm so sorry that he hurt so much. You are safe now. It's 3.47 am. You have time to sleep.

Reena: I want to stay awake now.

Zuby: You must sleep for your health.

Reena: OK.

Zuby: Then go back, please. Go to the compassionate mindset. I'm here if you need me.

Day Forty-seven
We met up after work and had a brief discussion about how awful she felt. When we departed she said she felt better but, as always, we would continue to text later.

Zuby: Make a start; talk to me.

Reena: I'll be ill.

Zuby: No, you won't, because you'll remind yourself how to dissociate.

Reena: It makes me sick; he did it because I looked like I was growing up. It reminds me of other things he did for that same reason 🤢.

Zuby: So now dissociate. You're finally accepting that you were a victim of a paedophile. You don't need to try harder to be a better person anymore. You don't need to please anyone. You're already good enough and you always were.

Reena: Yes.

Zuby: Tell me what he is.

Reena: I can't.

Zuby: Please try.

Reena: He's a paedophile.

Zuby: Paedophile – means all the evil, all the wrong things, all the negatives, the blame, the fault and the shame is his. You can let go of it.

Reena: I know but tbh I wasn't in a position to think or reflect on what he was doing. I didn't realise why he was doing it then. He hurt me a lot and each time I made excuses and thought that would be the last time and then convinced myself that it wasn't as bad as it had seemed in the moment.

Zuby: He did hurt you a lot. Excuses?

Reena: That he was drunk, that I could have stopped it getting that far, that he didn't mean to do it that badly, that maybe he didn't realise because I hadn't made it clear, that he won't do it again.

Zuby: But you know that none of that is true now?

Reena: Yes.

Day Forty-eight

Nightmare.

> Reena: I know it's over, I really do, but I really don't want to remember everything so vividly; it hurts all over again, it's not fair. I've survived it once; I don't want to be tortured by it again. It hurts. Five years ago this week could have helped all of this, but instead I was painted as a teenager with a crush. I'm trying to be a good person. I don't want all of these images and memories in my head. They hurt all over again and it's not fair. I'm upset at the vivid memories then I'm cross.

Zuby: You're upset and anger is understandable. It's real and it's justified because what happened was all wrong.

> Reena: It isn't fair. I've done my surviving and escaping, I know. But what happened is really, really rubbish and it really hurts. I'm not a toy but that's all I was for so long. It genuinely physically hurts today and it's stupid. I didn't have anyone to go to so I had to stay even though being homeless would have probably been better. I can't do this anymore.

Zuby: You're right in everything you say. It was a huge injustice and it was cruel. You did survive, that is why you have a home, are independent, free and safe. The physical hurt today feels genuine but it's not real because you are safe. We are working on removing that.

> Reena: I was OK yesterday; I managed. Why does today feel harder?

Zuby: It's harder because you had a tough day yesterday and we didn't talk about things. You probably would have got these feelings out yesterday. Currently, the greatest focus of upset for you is pain. I think this is understandable because this is one of the areas of neglect when you were a child. We have acknowledged fear, worth and shame but never pain. You weren't allowed to express it then and you still haven't. It's time to accept and acknowledge that part, have it validated and move into the present.

> Reena: I'm upset because it hurt and he decided I was worthless.

Zuby: He treated you as worthless but he knew that you were too good for him. He knew it was him that was worthless. The research shows that people like him hate themselves and project their self-hate onto their victim. He knows what he is and you drove that home when you left him. He's a pathetic excuse of a human being and he knows it. People like him cover it with bravado and by controlling another.

> Reena: I understand.

Zuby: What happened to you was wicked and unfair. He was inhumane towards you. He used you for his sexual pleasure. He was a sadist and deliberately hurt you even though his brainwashing would have got him what he wanted without resistance. He took away your dignity, allowing you no privacy at all. He violated and frightened you into total submission. Then you fought back and took control. You have rewired and have better understanding than ever before. You are the strongest person I know. I'm so proud of you. I know you will keep progressing and your life will be a happy, worthwhile one.

Reena: I am so much better than I was. Thank you.

Nightmares, flashbacks and then panic attacks – this illness was merciless. One day she had gone shopping and unexpectedly texted me.

Reena: Yes, sooru I dudmu mesn to

Zuby: It's OK. You're safe. Breathe.

Reena: Yrs

Zuby: Yes, tell me about you in the present.

Reena: Dafe

Zuby: Again.

Reena: Safe.

Zuby: Yes. What else?

            Reena: Knoelehe knowlehe

Zuby: Again.

              Reena: Knoeledge

Zuby: It's OK. I promise.

             Reena: Know ledge

Zuby: Yes, you're safe and in control because you have all the knowledge and learning you have done.

                 Reena: Yes.

Zuby: Your panic attacks are there because you have an illogical feeling that you are unsafe, that he'll be there to hurt you. But he really can't. You've taken the power back.

       Reena: Why does my own brain insist that I suffer again? I'm all out of fight. It helped but right now there's too many new dreams and my head will explode.

Zuby: You're wrong. You've had new dreams before.

           Reena: Then I'm just weaker.

Zuby: You don't believe in yourself.

Reena: I'm telling you I'm struggling; that's all I'm telling you.

Zuby: You have to focus on the fact that you are safe now. The memories aren't going to surprise. We know the feelings they evoke. It's time to shift to better coping strategies. Then the dreams will stop.

Reena: Understood.

Zuby: You're safe and in control. You can access your compassionate mindset so that you soothe and heal (instead of attack) yourself.

Reena: And it is all so much better than it was.

We watched a movie together. She fell asleep and had a reliving experience and, as I watched her, she woke up screaming and I calmed her. Once she was better, I went home and we texted again.

Zuby: Which one was it? What did you say yes to? (Please don't say if it's too upsetting).

Reena: I don't remember saying yes?

Zuby: You said 'Go away', you said 'Please stop' and you said 'Yes'. All several times. He hurt you and I could tell.

Reena: Oh, I was speaking to myself. I often said things in my head to get me through; sometimes I said them out loud but only ever very quietly.

Zuby: Yes, you did speak very quietly.

Reena: That's what it was, then.

Zuby: I don't understand. You said yes in your head?

Reena: Sorry, he went away part way through hurting me and I thought he was done.

Zuby: You grounded quickly. We're getting there.

Reena: Thank you for insisting, believing in me and for not giving up.

She went to a shopping centre and unfortunately she suffered another panic attack.

Reena: Can't do it.

Zuby: What?

Reena: Shop.

Zuby: Take 10 to breathe then go to your compassionate mindset.

No response…

Zuby: Are you already there?

Reena: Been in and come back.

Zuby: Are you in the carpark?

Reena: Yee Yes. I hate this.

Zuby: OK, just stop and breathe. You'll be able to overcome this. You're safe and in control.

I had to talk her through until she was able to catch her breath and stop crying. She decided to go home and leave the shopping for another time. Once home we resumed texting.

Zuby: I'm so proud of you today, fighting the panic attacks and refusing to give up. When I ask you to do those things, to challenge yourself, it is because I believe in you.

Reena: Thank you.

Zuby: You're healthy, young, capable and independent. You have the potential for a happy future. You really do. But you were right, this is your personal history; it will never change, but I promise you – with your determination and strength – your present and future will be your focus.

Reena: Thank you.

Zuby: Everything that happened is horrific; I don't dispute that for a second. But, to enjoy what you have earned and achieved, you can control the re-experiencing of it. You can and you have to learn not to experience all of it again. Please, please.

Reena: I will try.

Zuby: If there's a flashback, if there's a strong emotion – it's all valid but not helpful or useful now. Fight each and every negative emotion because you are free and safe. That's all that matters.

Day Forty-nine

Reena: We had a breakthrough yesterday, finally all the shame has gone – you did that.

Zuby: We did it. Couldn't be happier for you 🧸 🧸.

Reena: I knew what you have been doing was right; I could feel it. I'm glad the counselling confirmed it but I felt safe with you. I knew already.

Zuby: You were genuinely happy. It was heart-warming to see.

Reena: It's still scary being me right now. The flashbacks are cruel and the flashes startle me. It's not fair; I survived it once. Why do I need tormenting again?

Zuby: The biggest part has gone – the shame. That weight – it's still gone, right?

Reena: Yes. I understand. The rest will now go.

Zuby: Thank you for talking that through with me. I hope it will help. You did really well and you spoke about your feelings. Keep talking, processing. This will stop.

Reena: It feels better.

Zuby: Even during the flashbacks and dreams, you really, really are safe. I promise.

Reena: Thank you.

Re-experiencing the most horrific episodes left Reena unable to function sufficiently to enable herself to feel safe into the present. She would text me but, often, even that became a struggle. The routine became familiar; we knew what would work.

Reena: Wgat tomr woll youbib8w mornibf

Zuby: It's OK, you're safe and in your own home.

Reena: He told me he was going to be 'that guy'. I knew he was going to hurt me but I froze. I hate that he told me beforehand the persona he was going to adopt.

Zuby: It's bad enough he hurt you, but this means he intended to hurt you and he wanted you to know what was coming. He wanted to see how you'd react to knowing what he was about to do. He wanted you to be afraid. He got something out of that. I don't know why that makes it even worse but somehow it does.

Reena: I know it does. That's the nastiness I get upset about.

Zuby: This shows he made a choice to hurt and terrify. He wasn't out of control; in fact he was very calculating. He was truly sadistic. He would tell you before he hurt you. It was so deliberate and calculated. He wanted to watch as he told you because he enjoyed your reaction. It's sick.

> Reena: I understand. I suppose it would be easier to accept if he couldn't help it. But you're right; he was in control with others, whenever he wanted to be. 😔 Yes, this is why I get so upset.

Zuby: The truth is he was exerting power over a person who was physically weaker, anyway. He was a coward in every sense of the word.

> Reena: It didn't feel like he was a coward.

Zuby: It felt like he was all-powerful?

> Reena: Yes.

Zuby: Because he brainwashed you. But only a coward exerts power over a weaker person.

> Reena: I understand now, I'm just saying that back then that's what it felt like. I was scared, I knew what was going to happen but he'd not done it with that in his hand before.

Zuby: It's safe to say it any way you feel… Your words are valuable and respected.

Reena: Really?

Zuby: I'm still listening and I'm telling you your reactions were normal.

Reena: He hit me with it and kicked me from my knees and pushed me in the room.

Zuby: You said he told you what to do. You couldn't refuse and you know why?

Reena: Really scared, really upset, really hurting.

Zuby: That's totally understandable. Those are normal, natural reactions to that awful situation. Do you want to go on?

Reena: He carried on. I thought 'This is it, he's going to kill me'.

Zuby: You were terrified.

Reena: Yes.

Zuby: You remember every word and action, don't you?

Reena: Yes.

Zuby: You survived this and you're courageous enough to deal with it. He wanted you to react with fear so that he could feel powerful.

Reena: I wanted to run. I couldn't even scream.

Zuby: Because you froze. He thought you were being defiant. I totally validate how you felt. It was wrong that he denied your feelings. You were in survival mode so you couldn't scream or shout.

Reena: I tried to speak and to move. He growled 'Do I have to f****** do everything my f****** self?'

Zuby: I'm so, so sorry.

Reena: I'm sorry; I'll stop.

Zuby: No, I want you to have a voice. You have a right to be heard as well as validated. To know that this was unacceptable.

Reena: I stayed on the floor. I couldn't pick myself up. I just curled up.

Zuby: You did pick yourself up. You're amazing.

Reena: Thank you.

Zuby: You have all the learning you need from this memory – enough to keep you safe in the present. This memory can go now. Can you move into the present now where you really are safe? Where you are cared for and respected?

No answer.

Zuby: Do you feel any relief from the talking?

Reena: Yes.

Zuby: You did so well. You have finally verbalised your trauma. You verbalised in a way you haven't before. You have acknowledged yourself.

Meanwhile, people at work are cruel and accuse us of favouritism.

> Reena: I'm laying my cards on the table with the secret hope that no one actually reads this part 🤞 :
> - Why am I fundraising for a mental health charity? Why not something 'more serious'?
>
> Here's why:
> - Mental health has had such stigma attached to it for so long that when my own mental health began to suffer, I felt ashamed of myself.
> - Being ashamed wasn't something that was new to me. I was a straight A student (16 to be exact 😄), with A levels, a degree, a PGCE, was working in my dream job and generally the class clown of my own class. What could I possibly have to whinge about – right? The truth is that those accomplishments didn't come without a few hiccups and hurdles, just as many people have found throughout their lives. I took it in my stride and 'managed' or so I thought…
> - Then it hit me – complete and utter toxic shame for something that had happened to me years ago, nothing I played a part in or could possibly be blamed for, but that didn't seem to matter – I was utterly ashamed and I could not shift it.
> - I couldn't focus, I idealised suicide, I didn't want to leave my home or socialise and I barely

wanted to go into a job that I utterly adored. I was suffering with complex PTSD, but I hadn't been in a war zone. That's something soldiers get, isn't it? Well, after hours upon hours of research it turns out not.

Zuby: You've really made me understand. You are courageous enough to say what needs to be said. I really do understand. Today, though I know you are getting better and that you won't give up, I just need you to convince your subconscious of everything you know consciously. It is alright for you to feel whatever you feel. You don't need to turn on yourself for feeling sad. It's OK to, and it's understandable. Your mind is trying to tell you that you're hurting and you must acknowledge that.

Reena: I know, both. I am having some chinks of shorter sleep without nightmares.

Zuby: Really?

Reena: Yes.

Zuby: That's amazing.

Reena: (happy tears).

Zuby: How do you feel?

Reena: Like I want to give my friend the biggest squeeze ever.

Zuby: Me, too. This has to be the beginning of the
end.

Reena: I think I'm ready to write those letters now.

During the therapy sessions, it had been suggested that writing a
very honest letter to each of those that hurt her most would be of
help. Reena finally wrote her letter and, after discussion, she sent me
the one she would go on to send to her estranged parents.

Zuby: 'Dear…
I am a survivor. I have learned about myself and
about those around me through the experts I have
seen.
In 2004, I became the victim of a predatory
paedophile. I was systematically 'groomed' by
an individual who had access to me because my
main caregivers were neglectful; failing to parent
me by warning me of the potential dangers and
vulnerabilities a child has, and failing to supervise
me for up to 8 hours a day. True that I lied about
my whereabouts, but that was because of the
manipulative guidance of an adult male who saw an
opportunity in a 12-year-old girl, who longed for the
attention her family didn't afford her. My caregivers
failed to check and monitor my movements during
those days; I've learned that most families would
phone, drop off, pick up and check where their child
was and certainly wouldn't give them free rein at
that tender age.
In the years that followed, the same caregivers
handed me over to live with him, knowing that he
had broken the law by committing statutory rape – I

was just 15.

He subjected me to physical, verbal and sexual abuse with sadistic excess that would leave me suffering with complex post-traumatic stress disorder.

My family, knowing of his physical aggression towards me at the very least, remained aloof. After an attempted suicide, when faced with returning to him and terrified to do it myself, I asked my mother to speak in front of him to simply say – "Come home with me".

Her response – "I can't just do that" led to 2 more years of torture.

When finally, at 18, I took control and fled, my mother said "You got yourself into it but you've got yourself out of it, too". Throughout, my father's 'support' consisted of persistent name-calling and nothing more. Such actions and words strengthened the perpetrator's voice and reinforced hate and toxic shame in myself.

Finally free, I blocked out the past and carried on with my life until, years later, when the trigger finally hit and a hellish year began. Desperate to put things right and to bring an end to the hate I had for myself, I asked my family to be there for me. I asked what it was that I could do to become a better person so that my caregivers would finally accept me, inclusive of my past. This opportunity to help me heal was rejected by them yet again. I told them about the importance of my past and how I felt responsible. They chose not to engage, which affirmed my self-hate and to warn a friend of the dangers I presented. So, again, my caregivers failed

me and refused to help me, refused to accept me
or even to acknowledge my hurt. Instead I was left
alone. But for the compassion of a stranger, I would
not be here today.

Now I'm educated about the past; I know it wasn't
my fault – I was just a child. The fault, the shame,
the blame is his and my caregivers, who normalised
domestic violence in my early years and then
redoubled my ordeal, adding to my trauma by
never, not to this day, accepting me enough to allow
me a voice.

Day by day, I'm accepting myself and healing. I'm a
survivor and I'm beginning to thrive.'

Zuby: You are healing, you are getting stronger, you
are buying a house and you'll make it into a home.
You can plan to have children and you will feel the
joys of being a mum. That is genuinely a possibility.
You've finally had your say and when you send it to
them – you will be heard.

> Reena: Couldn't have seen that coming a year ago
> today. Well done you.

Zuby: See what you can do? All you ever needed
was guidance and love.

> Reena: Please don't think of me as that hurt girl
> anymore. Just the healed person you helped me to
> become.

Day Fifty

Despite focusing on work talk only, as I had instructed, formally close colleagues continued to lack any compassion towards Reena. I explained how she was making a good recovery due to her engagement with the services. She apologised for the impact of her mental illness on others, the episode she had had, but now that it was over she was improving. Frustratingly, they made her life unbearable at work.

> Reena: I haven't done anything wrong and I haven't for a long time. I've bent over backwards to prove that to everyone and I'm sick. I'm not doing any more, I shouldn't have to and I won't. I'm clearly not going to be allowed to build my career. You've never done anything wrong at all so you shouldn't have to change anything, either.

Zuby: You and I both work hard and do our best –
end of.

> Reena: Rosey caught me as I was on the way in, she's really impressed with your not taking any sh*t speech x

Zuby: ☺ 🧸 🧸 Enough is enough. Got more important things to deal with, right?

> Reena: She was very impressed with your dealing of a lunch issue. I'll never be able to repay you.

Zuby: You will – just by making me proud by continuing to do what you're doing.

Reena: You don't know what your words mean x thank you. I don't know what to say.

Zuby: Say you know your worth; that you know who you are and what you want to be. Say you are strong enough to make your choices and say that you know that that will make you happy.

Reena: And I've fought really bloody hard for a long time and I've won.

Zuby: You're talking like you actually believe it, like I always have.

Reena: I do.

Zuby: You've been different since you found out about work and since you wrote your letter.

Reena: I found strength. I know what I want to do; I can put my energy into that. You've carried, guided and taught a very lost person who didn't even know who she was and couldn't move beyond the past. And today she can honestly tell you she is living in the present, knows what she wants in the future and has the strength and knowledge to make it happen.

Reena: Because you're amazing, it would have been so much easier and completely understandable for you to walk away because it was too big, but you didn't. You read every article, every book and estimation of when this would all be over.

Zuby: You've done it and you deserve to be OK now, you deserve to be content. You should never have had your life changed and altered by it all in the first place. We can't share those conversations, those tears, with anyone else. So we have a special bond. That makes us family. You are good enough. They are supposed to have compassion in bucket-loads. I'm shocked by their lack of understanding of mental health.

> Reena: They scare me – I'm never going to be good enough.

Zuby: You don't need to please anyone or fit in with their expectations. You didn't do anything wrong. Not then and not now. I understand you need time now. It's not that it's 'fixed' and that's the end of it…

> Reena: Zuby,

Zuby: What?

> Reena: I think I'm happy. I know who I am and what I have control of – more importantly I know what I can let go of. My friends are genuine and I love my career. I know the things I really want from life, they're possible and I know I can get there. My family won't acknowledge my past so I'm to cut myself free from them – it's safer for me.

Zuby: Why now?

Reena: Because happiness isn't about waiting to get something or somewhere. It's about realising what you have in the present and how fortunate that is. I can't believe we're here x I can't believe we made it 😢.

Zuby: We've gone from one crisis to the next for a year. It's been intense. Exhausting.

Reena: I'm happy. I'm happy now but that doesn't mean it won't really hurt sometimes, cut really deep and make me want to scream. But I'm still happy now!

It had taken us almost two years of intense, uncompromising determination and friendship that changed both our lives forever. The days improved and became full of the usual things friends do. We raised money for mental health support and walked together when the weather was good. Days remained where it appeared that she had slipped again. The betrayal by those she had considered friends or family, but who decided at her time of need to call her a liar or to abandon her, caused her deep hurt. The lack of acceptance of those she loved slowed the healing but we recognised that this would be a long path. It was so much better and the future finally seemed worth the chase – each day something to look forward to and new memories worth making.

END

REFERENCES

1. 'Instead of seeing ourselves as a problem to be fixed... SELF-kindness/compassion allows us to see ourselves as valuable human beings who are worthy of care.' Kristen Neff

2. 'I'm a survivor. I want acknowledgement, receptivity and understanding. I just want someone to sit over there and listen to me…I need my story to be witnessed, and that's the validation I'm looking for.' Visible Project

3. 'Shame is the lie someone told you about yourself.' Anais Nin

4. 'It may feel like there are a million reasons to stand still and keep silent, but there are millions more to speak the unspeakable and move forward.' Ellen Hendriksen PhD, *Psychology Today*

5. 'A moment of self-compassion can change your entire day. A string of such moments can change the course of your life.' Christopher K Germer

www.ingramcontent.com/pod-product-compliance
Lightning Source LLC
Chambersburg PA
CBHW032221190726
48289CB00007BA/2340